P9-CAP-880

CHICKEN CHICKEN

Look for more Goosebumps books
by R.L. Stine:
(see back of book for a complete listing)

Goosebumps®

CHICKEN CHICKEN

R.L. STINE

AN
APPLE
PAPERBACK

SCHOLASTIC INC.
New York Toronto London Auckland Sydney

A PARACHUTE PRESS BOOK

If you purchased this book without a cover, you should be aware that this book is stolen property. It was reported as "unsold and destroyed" to the publisher, and neither the author nor the publisher has received any payment for this "stripped book."

No part of this publication may be reproduced in whole or in part, or stored in a retrieval system, or transmitted in any form or by any means, electronic, mechanical, photocopying, recording, or otherwise, without written permission of the publisher. For information regarding permission, write to Scholastic Inc., 555 Broadway, New York, NY 10012.

ISBN 0-590-56890-6

Copyright © 1997 by Parachute Press, Inc.
All rights reserved. Published by Scholastic Inc.
APPLE PAPERBACKS and the APPLE PAPERBACKS logo are registered trademarks of Scholastic Inc.
GOOSEBUMPS is a registered trademark of Parachute Press, Inc.

12 11 10 9 8 7 6 5 4 3 2 1   7 8 9/9 0 1 2/0

Printed in the U.S.A.   40

First Scholastic printing, March 1997

CHICKEN CHICKEN

I hate chickens.

They are filthy creatures, and they smell like . . . like . . . chickens.

"Crystal, it's your turn to feed the chickens," Mom says. My least favorite words.

I carry the seed bucket out to the backyard, and they come scurrying over, clucking and squawking and flapping their greasy wings. I hate the way they brush up against my legs as they peck the seeds off the ground. Their feathers are so rough and scratchy.

My brother, Cole, and I are always trying to convince my parents to get rid of the chickens. "Just because we live on a farm doesn't mean we have to have chickens," I always say.

"Right! We're not farmers!" Cole agrees. "So why do we have to have those smelly chickens?"

"It's always been our dream," Mom always replies. Blah blah blah.

Cole and I have heard the dream story a thousand times.

We've heard how Mom and Dad grew up in the Bronx in New York City. How they hated the noise and the dirt and the concrete. How they dreamed of leaving the city for good and living on a farm near a small country town.

So, when Cole was two and I was four, we moved to Goshen Falls. Lucky us! The whole town is three blocks long. We have a cute little farm with a cute little farmhouse. And even though Mom and Dad are computer programmers — not farmers — we have a backyard full of chickens.

Cluck. Cluck. That's *their* dream.

My dream is that Cole gets punished for mouthing off the way he always does. And his punishment is that *he* has to feed the chickens for the rest of his life.

Everyone has to have a dream — right?

"OWW!" A chicken pecked my ankle. That hurt! Their beaks are so sharp.

I tossed a final handful of seed on the ground and hopped backward, away from the gross, clucking creatures. Their little black eyes glinted in the sunlight as they strutted over the grass. Pecking each other. Bumping each other out of the way as they dipped their scrawny heads for the food.

2

I dropped the bucket in the back of the little barn we also use as a garage. Then I washed my hands under the cold water spigot at the side of the barn.

I heard a low roar. A shadow rolled over the barn. I gazed up to see a small plane dipping under the puffy afternoon clouds.

I took a deep breath. The tangy aroma of potatoes floated in the air.

That's what the farmers grow around here. Mostly potatoes and corn.

I dried my hands on the legs of my jeans and hurried off in search of my brother. It was a sunny Saturday afternoon. Most of my friends from school were away on a 4-H club trip.

Mom asked me to keep an eye on Cole. He's ten, two years younger than me. But sometimes he acts like a four-year-old. It seems like he's always finding new ways to get into trouble.

I wandered through town. No sign of him. I asked Mrs. Wagner at the bakery if she'd seen him. Cole likes to stop in there and beg her for free doughnuts.

Mrs. Wagner said she saw Cole and his friend Anthony heading out of town in the direction of Pullman's Pond.

Uh-oh, I thought. What are they planning to do at the pond? I started to the door.

"I just love your hair, Crystal," Mrs. Wagner

3

called. "It's such a beautiful deep shade of red. You should be a model. Really. You're so tall and thin."

"Thanks, Mrs. Wagner!" I called as the door closed behind me. I wasn't thinking about my hair or being a model. I was thinking about Cole and Anthony and the pond.

I trotted the rest of the way through town. Waved to Mr. Porter standing in the window of the Pic 'n' Pay. Then I turned off the street and followed the dirt path that led to Pullman's Pond.

I didn't have to go far to find Cole and Anthony. They were hiding behind the long hedge at the edge of Vanessa's property.

I gazed beyond the hedge to the falling-down old farmhouse where Vanessa lives.

Who is Vanessa? I guess you might say she is the most interesting person in Goshen Falls. And the most weird.

Actually, Vanessa is like someone from a horror movie. She is kind of pretty, with long, straight black hair and a pale, white face. She dresses all in black. She wears black lipstick and black fingernail polish.

Vanessa is a mystery woman. No one knows if she's young or old.

She keeps to herself. I've hardly ever seen her in town. She lives in her old farmhouse right outside of town with her black cat.

Naturally, everyone says she is some kind of sorceress.

4

I've heard all kinds of stories about Vanessa. Frightening stories. Most of the kids in Goshen Falls are scared of her. But that doesn't stop them from playing tricks on her.

Kids are always daring each other to sneak up to Vanessa's house. It's kind of a game everyone plays. Sneak up to her house, tap on the window, make her cat screech. Then run away before Vanessa sees you.

"Hey — Cole!" I called in a loud whisper. I ducked my head as I ran along the hedge. If Vanessa was home, I didn't want her to see me.

"Hey, Cole — what's up?"

As I came nearer, I saw that Cole and Anthony weren't alone. Two other kids huddled behind the hedge. Franny Jowett and Jeremy Garth.

Cole raised a finger to his lips. "Ssshhhh. Vanessa is in there."

"What are you doing?" I demanded. I saw that Franny and Jeremy held plastic water pitchers in their hands. "Is that lemonade or something?"

They shook their heads solemnly.

"Some kids dared them to fill Vanessa's mailbox with water," Cole explained.

"Huh?" I gasped. I stared at Franny and Jeremy. "You're not going to do it — are you?"

"They have to," Cole answered for them. "A dare is a dare."

"But that's so mean!" I protested.

My brother snickered. "The mailbox is right

5

next to the front door. No way they won't get caught."

Franny and Jeremy are blond and pale. Now they looked even paler than usual. Jeremy made a soft, choking sound. Franny gripped her pitcher tightly and peered over the hedge at the black metal mailbox on its tilted pole.

"You accepted the dare. Are you going to wimp out?" Cole demanded.

Franny and Jeremy glanced at each other nervously. They didn't reply.

"Don't do it," Anthony suddenly chimed in.

We all turned to Anthony. He's short and chubby and has a round face and very short black hair. He wears red-framed glasses that are always slipping down his little pug nose.

"Don't do it," Anthony repeated.

"Why n-not?" Franny stammered.

"Didn't you hear what happened when Vanessa caught Tommy Pottridge?" Anthony asked in a hushed whisper. "Didn't you hear what she did to him?"

"No!" Franny and Jeremy declared together.

I felt a tremble of fear run down my back. "What did Vanessa do to Tommy?" I demanded.

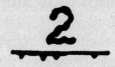

2

I peered over the tall hedge. Did something move in Vanessa's front window?

No. Just a glint of sunlight on the windowpane.

We huddled closer to Anthony. Even though it was a warm spring day, I suddenly felt chilled. "What did Vanessa do to Tommy?" I repeated in a whisper.

"She caught him sneaking up to her house," Anthony reported. "She did some kind of magic spell on him. She made his head blow up like a balloon."

"Oh, come on!" I exclaimed, rolling my eyes.

"No — really!" Anthony protested. "His head was huge. And it got all soft and squishy. Like a sponge."

Cole laughed.

Anthony clamped a hand over Cole's mouth. "It's true!" he insisted. "Vanessa gave him a big, soft, spongy head. That's why we don't see Tommy around anymore!"

"But the Pottridges moved away!" Franny cried.

"That's why they moved," Anthony replied. "Because of Tommy's head."

We all froze for a moment, thinking about Anthony's story. I tried to picture Tommy with a big, squishy head.

Cole broke the silence. "Give me that!" he cried. He grabbed the water pitcher from Jeremy's hands. "*I'll* fill up her mailbox. I'm not scared."

"No way!" Jeremy protested. He wrestled the pitcher away from my brother. Then he turned to Franny. "We're doing it — right? We were dared, so we have to do it — right?"

Franny swallowed hard. "I guess," she choked out.

"All right!" Cole cheered, slapping them both on the back. Franny nearly dropped her pitcher. "You can do it! Lots of kids play tricks on Vanessa. And they don't get squishy heads."

"I still think it's mean to fill someone's mailbox with water," I protested. "And it's not worth the risk."

No one wanted to listen to me or my warnings.

Franny and Jeremy tiptoed to the end of the hedge. Then they began slowly making their way over the tall, weed-choked grass.

They carried their plastic water pitchers in both hands in front of them. And they kept their eyes on the tilted mailbox to the right of the front door of Vanessa's farmhouse.

Cole, Anthony, and I crept out from behind the hedge to watch. I held my breath and stared at the front window, looking out for Vanessa.

But the glare of yellow sunlight filled the windowpane. I couldn't see a thing.

Franny and Jeremy seemed to be moving in slow motion. It was taking them *forever* to cross the lawn to the mailbox!

A million tiny white gnats flew over the tall grass. Swirling and dancing in the sunlight, the gnats sparkled like jewels.

Franny and Jeremy walked right through them. Their eyes didn't leave the mailbox.

The two boys and I stepped a little closer, eager to see better.

No sign of anyone inside the house.

We stepped even closer.

At last, Jeremy pulled down the metal mailbox lid. He and Franny raised their plastic pitchers.

They both lowered the pitchers to the mailbox.

And poured.

The water made a soft splashing sound as it hit the metal mailbox.

Franny emptied her pitcher. Jeremy had nearly emptied his.

Then the front door swung open — and Vanessa burst out.

She wore a flowing black dress. Her straight

black hair flew wildly behind her. Her black-lipsticked lips were open in an angry cry.

The cat screeched shrilly from somewhere in the house.

Franny dropped her pitcher. She bent to pick it up.

Changed her mind.

Ran.

Jeremy was already diving into the bushes at the far side of the house. Franny ran close behind him.

Cole, Anthony, and I hadn't moved.

We stood in the grass. Frozen. Watching Vanessa.

I gasped when I saw Vanessa's furious stare.

I turned to Cole and Anthony. "Why is she staring like that at *us?*" I choked out. "Does she think *we* did it?"

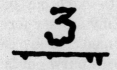

3

My whole body stiffened. As if Vanessa's eyes were shooting out some kind of laser ray.

I forced myself to spin away. And I started to run.

Cole and Anthony were at my sides. Our sneakers thudded heavily over the dirt path. We kicked up clouds of dirt as we ran. A blur of green and brown, the fields appeared to tilt and sway around me.

We ran through town without stopping. Without saying a word. Without even *looking* at each other!

Mrs. Wagner stepped out of the bakery. She started to say hello. I caught the shocked expression on her face as the three of us ran past her without slowing down.

We ran until we reached my house. We burst through the gate, slamming it open so hard, the whole fence shook. I pushed open the front door with my shoulder, and all three of us staggered into the living room.

Gasping for breath, I dropped to my knees on the carpet.

Cole and Anthony collapsed onto the couch.

We struggled to catch our breath. I brushed my hair back off my sweaty forehead. The clock on the mantel chimed. Three o'clock.

Cole and Anthony burst out laughing.

I narrowed my eyes at them. "What's so funny?" I demanded breathlessly.

That made them laugh even harder.

"What's so funny, guys?" I repeated. I climbed to my feet and pressed my hands into my waist, waiting for an answer. "Why are you laughing?"

"I don't know!" Cole answered finally.

"I don't know, either!" Anthony echoed.

And they both laughed again.

"You're crazy," I muttered, shaking my head. "That wasn't funny. It was scary."

Cole pulled himself up. His expression turned serious. "Did you see the way Vanessa stared at us?"

"She didn't see Franny and Jeremy," Anthony said. "She only saw us." He pulled off his glasses and cleaned them on his T-shirt sleeve. The short black hair on his round head glistened with sweat.

I felt a chill. "What if Vanessa decides to do

12

something terrible to us?" I demanded. "You two won't be laughing then."

Cole pulled himself up even straighter. He ran a hand back through his wavy blond hair. Cole is tall and even skinnier than me. Sometimes I think he looks like a grasshopper.

"Crystal, what do you mean?" he demanded softly.

"I mean, if Vanessa thinks *we* were the ones who filled her mailbox with water, maybe she'll pay *us* back. You know. Make our heads swell up or something."

"But we didn't do anything!" Anthony protested. "We have to tell her it was Franny and Jeremy."

"Snitch," Cole muttered, grinning at his friend.

"Maybe she won't give us a chance to explain," I said. "Maybe she'll just do something horrible to us."

I started to the kitchen. "You guys want something to drink?"

I didn't hear their replies.

I pulled open the fridge and took out a bottle of iced tea.

A second later, I opened my mouth in a loud scream of pain.

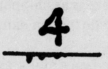

4

"Crystal — what happened?" Cole came running into the kitchen.

I shuddered in pain. "Ohhhh."

"What *happened?*" he cried.

I shook my hand, trying to shake away the throbbing. "The fridge door," I managed to choke out. "I — slammed it on my hand."

I shook my hand some more. Then I tested each finger. I could move them. Nothing broken.

I raised my eyes to Cole. "Why are you grinning?" I demanded.

"You didn't slam your hand," he replied. "Vanessa did!"

Anthony giggled from the doorway.

"Cole — you're not funny!" I screeched. I wrapped my fingers around his scrawny neck and pretended to strangle him. But my hand still hurt. I had to let go.

"Vanessa cursed you," Anthony said, picking

up where Cole had left off. "Now your hand will probably swell up to the size of a cantaloupe."

"And it will get soft and squishy like Tommy's head," Cole added gleefully. "Soft and squishy — like your *brain!*"

"Not funny! Not funny!" I insisted. I admit it. I felt a little afraid. I didn't like kidding around about this stuff.

My hand ached and burned. I opened the freezer and stuck it inside. "What if Vanessa really *has* powers?" I asked them. "What if she really did make me slam the door on my hand?"

Cole and Anthony raised their hands in front of them and began moving them back and forth, as if casting spells on me. "You are a *sponge head!*" Cole cried, lowering his voice, trying to sound like a real sorcerer. "You will mop up the dinner dishes with your head!"

That's when Mom and Dad walked in.

"What on earth — ?" Mom cried. "Crystal — why do you have your hand in the freezer?"

"Oh. Uh . . ." I slid my hand out and closed the freezer door. "Just cooling off," I said.

Mom narrowed her eyes at me. "Cooling off one hand?"

"Actually, I slammed a door on it," I told her.

"Vanessa slammed a door on it," Cole corrected.

"Vanessa?" Dad asked, crossing to the sink.

"You mean that strange woman who lives outside of town?"

"Have you been pestering that poor woman again?" Mom demanded. "Don't you kids have anything better to do than sneak around and play tricks on her?"

"We didn't do anything," Cole said. "Really."

"That's the truth," Anthony chimed in.

"Then why did you mention Vanessa?" Mom asked Cole.

I decided I'd better change the subject. "Where were you two?" I asked my parents.

"Out back. Trying to decide where to put the fence for the vegetable garden," Dad replied. He was washing his hands in the kitchen sink, something Mom always scolds him for.

"If we didn't have chickens, you wouldn't need a fence," I grumbled. "I think you should get rid —"

"That reminds me," Mom interrupted. "Cole, some of the chickens wandered all the way to the back. Would you go out and round them up, please?"

"Chicken Roundup!" I exclaimed gleefully. I slapped Cole on the back. "Congrats! Your favorite job!"

"But that's not fair! I did the chicken roundup last time!" Cole wailed. "It's Crystal's turn!"

"I fed them this morning," I declared. "And it

wasn't even my turn. Besides, it's easier for you to round them up. Because you look like a big rooster!"

Everyone laughed except Cole. He grumbled and shook his head. Then he grabbed Anthony and pulled him outside to help with the chicken roundup.

A few seconds later, I could hear a lot of clucking and squawking back there. And I could hear the boys shouting and complaining.

Did you ever try to herd chickens?

It isn't easy.

My hand ached all day from slamming it on the fridge door. And every time it ached, I thought of Vanessa.

And I pictured her cold eyes, staring at the boys and me.

She isn't going to do anything to us, I told myself. She *can't* do anything to us. Those stories about Vanessa can't be true.

I kept repeating this to myself. But that night, I had trouble falling asleep.

I kept seeing a shadow move against my bedroom wall. The shadow of a cat.

I climbed out of bed and pulled down the window blind. Now the room was bathed in total darkness. No shadows on the wall.

I still couldn't fall asleep.

I stared wide-eyed into the blackness.

"Crystal, go to sleep," I instructed myself. "You are scaring yourself for no reason."

A creaking sound made me jump.

A crack of gray light at my bedroom door.

Another creak — and the streak of light grew wider.

I swallowed hard.

I watched the door slowly slide open.

Staring in silence, I realized that someone was creeping into my bedroom.

Someone wearing a black veil. And a long black dress.

Vanessa!

5

I opened my mouth to scream. But only a low moan came out.

I started to jump out of bed. But where could I run?

She slid silently toward me, arms reaching out as if ready to grab me. Her face was hidden behind the heavy black veil.

How did she get in the house?

What is she going to do to me?

The frightening questions fluttered through my mind.

She leaned over my bed. Her hands moved to my throat.

"No!" I choked out.

I reached up. Pushed away her hands. Grasped her veil in both hands. And tugged it off.

Cole!

In the gray light from the open doorway, I could see his grin.

"Cole — you *jerk!*" I shrieked.

I tossed the veil down. Dove for him. Tried to tackle him to the floor.

But I missed — and tumbled out of bed.

"Cole — you creep! You scared me to death!"

I don't think he heard me over his gleeful laughter.

I scrambled to my feet. He dodged away from me. Still cackling, he backed up to the doorway. "You really thought it was Vanessa!" he cried.

"Did not!" I lied. "You just scared me, that's all."

"Did too!" he insisted. "You thought it was Vanessa. You really thought she had come to pay you back!"

"Did not! Did not!" I cried angrily.

He made hand motions as if casting a spell. "Abracadabra! You're a sponge head!"

He started laughing again. He really thought he was a riot.

"I'll pay you back!" I promised him. "Really. I'm going to pay you back!"

Shaking his head, he made his way out of the room, the long black skirt trailing over the floor. With an angry growl, I picked up the veil and heaved it after him.

I punched my pillow furiously. Why did I let him fool me like that? Now he'd tell everyone in school that I thought Vanessa was sneaking into my room.

My heart still pounding, I climbed back into

bed. I felt so angry, it took me hours to fall asleep. And when I finally drifted off, I dreamed about a cat.

An ugly black cat with bright yellow eyes and a bloodred tongue.

The cat hunched in an all-white room. But then the room became my room.

In the dream, the cat moved to the end of my bed. It opened its mouth wide. The bright red tongue darted over its yellow teeth.

And then the cat began to screech.

A sharp, painful sound — like fingernails dragged over a chalkboard.

It screeched. And screeched. Its mouth opened wider. Its yellow eyes flamed.

I couldn't stand the sound. In the dream, I saw myself cover my ears with both hands.

But the shrill screeching grew even louder.

The cat floated closer. Closer. Opened its jaws wide, as if to swallow me.

I woke up, stunned by the sudden silence.

The dream had been so real. I expected to see the screeching cat standing on my bedcovers.

Bars of yellow sunlight fell through the window blinds onto my floor. I saw the crumpled black veil beside the door.

No cat.

I stretched and climbed out of bed. Yawning, I got dressed for school.

Mom was setting down a bowl of cornflakes

and a glass of orange juice for me when I reached the kitchen. "Sleep well?" she asked.

"Not at all," I grumbled. I dropped into my seat at the breakfast table. "First I couldn't get to sleep. Then I had an annoying nightmare."

Mom tsk-tsked. She crossed to the sink and began pouring water into the coffeemaker.

I thought about telling her about Cole's dumb joke. But I decided not to. Mom would only start asking us again about what we were doing at Vanessa's house yesterday.

"What are you doing after school, Crystal?" she asked, clicking on the coffeemaker. "Maybe you can come home and rest up then."

"No way," I replied, swallowing a mouthful of cornflakes. "I've got basketball practice. Coach Clay says she's going to give me extra playing time. I told her how tired I am of being the *sixth* girl. I want to be a starter. But I never get enough playing time to show how good I am."

Mom turned to me. She blew a strand of brown hair off her forehead. "Maybe that's why you couldn't sleep last night," she said. "Maybe you were nervous about basketball practice."

I shrugged. I didn't want to tell her the real reason.

I heard Cole clomping down the stairs. Mom pulled out a cereal bowl for him.

"When are you going to buy a birthday present

for Lucy-Ann?" Mom asked me. "You know her birthday party is Saturday."

Lucy-Ann is one of my best friends. She has been talking about this birthday — her thirteenth! — for weeks. She's so excited about becoming a teenager.

"Maybe I'll go shopping tomorrow after school," I replied.

"What are you going to get her?"

I opened my mouth to answer, but Cole came charging into the room.

One look at his face — and Mom and I both gasped.

"Cole!" Mom cried.

"My f-face . . ." he stammered.

His cheeks and forehead were covered with big sores. Ugly red blotches.

"It . . . hurts . . ." he groaned. He turned to me. "Vanessa," he murmured. "Vanessa did this to me."

6

Cole dropped to his knees and covered his face with his hands.

I jumped up from my chair. "Cole — ?"

"I'll call the doctor!" Mom cried. "Or should I dial 911?" She bent over Cole. "Does it really hurt? Are you really in pain?"

Cole slowly lowered his hands. And as he did, I saw the broad grin on his face.

And I saw that his hands had smeared the red blotches on his cheeks.

"Cole!" I screamed furiously.

Mom's mouth dropped open. She had one hand on the phone, ready to call the doctor.

"Red marker pen," Cole said through his grin. Then he burst out laughing.

"Aaaagggh!" I let out a furious cry — and heaved my cereal spoon at him. It bounced off his chest and clattered across the linoleum floor.

"Not funny!" I screamed.

Mom shook her head. "Cole, you really scared me." She sighed.

Cole stood up and pointed at me. "Crystal, you really believed Vanessa did it to me," he accused.

"Your jokes are just stupid!" I cried. "I'm never going to believe you again. Even if you get hit by a truck, I won't believe you!"

I spun around and stormed out of the kitchen.

Behind me, I could hear Mom telling Cole, "You really have to stop scaring your sister."

"Why?" Cole asked.

I grabbed my backpack, tore out of the house, and slammed the door behind me.

I forced Vanessa from my mind.

I didn't think about her once that whole day.

In fact, I didn't think about her until the next time I saw her.

And that's when all the frightening stuff really started.

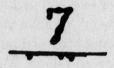

7

"Is that Lucy-Ann's cake?" Cole asked.

"Well, it says HAPPY BIRTHDAY, LUCY-ANN on it," I replied. "So what's *your* guess, genius?"

Cole, Anthony, and I had our noses pressed against the window of the bakery. Several white-frosted birthday cakes were on display. Lucy-Ann's stood in the middle of the shelf, ready to be picked up for her party on Saturday.

I saw Mrs. Wagner waving to us from behind the counter inside the store. I waved back to her. Then I checked my watch.

"Hey — I'm late," I told the boys. "I've got to buy a present for Lucy-Ann. Then I've got to get home and study my math."

I hurried toward the Mini-Mart on the corner next to the grocery. My plan was to buy Lucy-Ann a new CD. At the end of the block, Mr. Horace's old hound sprawled in the middle of Main

Street, lazily scratching his mangy ear with a back paw, looking as if he owned the town.

I heard Cole and Anthony laughing behind me. I turned and made a shooing motion with both hands. "Take a walk, guys. You don't have to tag along with me."

They ignored me, as usual.

Cole slipped an egg from his pocket. His eyes flashed mischievously. "Think fast!" he cried. He tossed the egg at Anthony.

Anthony cupped his hands and caught the egg. Without a pause, he tossed it back to my brother.

"Oh, please," I begged. "Not this stupid game."

Cole had to stretch — but he caught the egg in one hand.

This is one of their games that drives me crazy. They throw an egg back and forth, back and forth as they walk. Each time they throw it, they stand a little farther apart from each other.

The idea is to see how far they can toss the egg without breaking it.

The answer usually is: not too far.

One of them always ends up with egg splattered all over him. Once I made the mistake of trying to dive between them and intercept the egg. Too bad I intercepted it with my *forehead*.

"Please, guys," I begged. "Go do your egg toss somewhere else — okay?"

Cole backed up into the middle of the street. A

few feet away, Mr. Horace's old hound yawned and rolled onto his back. I saw two men in overalls pulling enormous burlap bags of feed from the Feed Store across the street.

"Yo!" Cole called — and heaved the egg high in the air.

Anthony raised a hand to shield his eyes from the sun. He backed up, back, back — nearly to the grocery store.

And the egg plopped down on top of his head.

What a disgusting *craaack* it made. Really gross.

"Huh?" Anthony uttered a startled gasp. And yellow goo started to flow down his forehead and the sides of his hair.

"Sorry. It got away from me!" Cole cried. But he couldn't keep a straight face. He burst out laughing.

Anthony let out an angry growl and charged at Cole.

Cole dodged away from him and ran up onto the sidewalk.

"Stop it! Stop it!" I shouted.

Roaring like an angry lion, Anthony dove at my brother and pinned him against the grocery store window. "You did that on purpose!" he shouted.

"No way! It was an accident!" Cole replied, laughing.

Anthony lowered his egg-gloppy head and head-butted Cole in the chest.

"Ooof!" My brother let out a groan.

Anthony pulled back his head and prepared another head butt.

Cole glanced down at his T-shirt. It was drenched in sticky egg yolk.

"Stop it! Stop it!" Shrieking at them, I dove between them. I grabbed Anthony's shoulders and tried to tug him off Cole.

I didn't see Vanessa step out of the grocery store.

None of us did.

"Get *off!*" I begged Anthony. I gave him a hard tug.

And all three of us bounced hard into Vanessa.

First I saw her black dress. Then I saw her pale face. Saw her dark eyes go wide with surprise.

I saw her mouth fall open. Her hands fly up.

And two bags of groceries bounced to the sidewalk.

I heard one bag rip. And I heard cans and bottles clatter onto the street.

The sound of shattering glass made me turn to the street. I saw a puddle of deep red ketchup that had leaked from a broken ketchup bottle. A carton of eggs lay open and shattered in the gutter.

I still had Anthony's shoulders gripped in both hands. A shiver ran down his body. He pulled free of me with a hard jerk.

"Sorry!" he cried to Vanessa. "I'm really sorry!"

Then he jumped over some of her groceries — and went running into the street.

"Whooooa!" Anthony cried out as he tripped over the hound dog. He went down face first on the pavement on top of the dog.

The dog didn't make a sound. It hardly moved.

Anthony struggled to his feet. Then he roared off behind the Feed Store. He disappeared without ever looking back.

"Oh, wow," I murmured, staring down at the ruined groceries all over the street. "Oh, wow."

Cole stood beside me, breathing noisily, shaking his head.

The dog loped over slowly, favoring one leg. He lowered his head and began licking egg yolk off the pavement.

I turned to Vanessa and nearly gasped when I saw the look of fury on her cold, pale face.

As her eyes locked on mine, I felt as if I'd been stabbed — by an icicle.

A shiver of fear made me take a step back. I grabbed Cole's arm. I started to pull him away.

But Vanessa stepped forward, her long black dress sweeping along the sidewalk. She pointed to Cole with a slender finger tipped in black nail polish. Then she pointed at me.

"Chicken chicken," she whispered.

A smile spread over Vanessa's black-lipsticked lips as she rasped those words at us.

"Chicken chicken."

I gasped as if I'd been slapped.

The street tilted in front of me. Then it started to spin.

What on earth did she mean? Why did she say that?

Cole and I didn't wait to ask her. Our sneakers thudded the pavement as we took off, running at full speed.

I glimpsed the old hound dog, still lapping up egg yolk from the street. And I glimpsed Vanessa's angry face for one more brief second.

And then Cole and I whipped around the corner, sped past the post office and the dry cleaner, and ran all the way home.

I didn't glance back once. And I didn't say a word until we were safely in the kitchen.

I collapsed onto a kitchen stool. Cole ran the

cold water in the sink and splashed it over his face and hair.

We were both panting and wheezing, too breathless to speak. I wiped the sweat off my forehead with my arm. Then I crossed to the fridge and pulled out a small bottle of water. Twisting off the cap, I tilted it to my mouth and drank it down.

"We should have stayed," I finally managed to sputter.

"Huh?" Cole turned to me. He had water dripping down his red face. The front of his T-shirt was soaked.

"We should have stayed and helped Vanessa pick up her groceries," I told him.

"No way!" Cole protested. "She's crazy! Did you see the look on her face?"

"Well . . . we knocked down all of her groceries," I said.

"So? It was an accident," my brother insisted. "Accidents happen all the time, right? But she . . . she wanted to *destroy* us!"

I rubbed the cool bottle against my pounding forehead. "Why did she say that to us?" I asked, thinking out loud. "Why did she whisper like that?"

Cole changed his expression. He reached out his hand and pointed a finger at me. Then he did a pretty good Vanessa imitation. "Chicken chicken!" he rasped, shaking his finger at me.

"Stop it!" I snapped. "I mean, really. Stop it, Cole. You're giving me the creeps."

"Chicken chicken," he whispered again.

"Come on. Give me a break," I pleaded. I crushed the plastic bottle in my hand. "It's just so weird," I murmured. "Why did she say that word? Why?"

Cole shrugged. "Because she's crazy?"

I shook my head fretfully. "She isn't crazy. She's evil," I said. I wrapped my arms around myself. "I just have this feeling that something horrible is going to happen now."

Cole rolled his eyes. "Crystal — what could happen?"

9

"Did you buy a present for Lucy-Ann?" Mom asked at dinner.

I swallowed a forkful of spaghetti. "Well . . . actually . . . no."

She gazed up at me in surprise. "But I thought you went into town to buy her a CD."

"Pass the Parmesan cheese," Dad interrupted. So far, those were his only words this evening. Guess he had a bad day at work.

"I don't understand," Mom insisted. "What did you do after school, Crystal?"

"Nothing, Mom." I sighed. "Can we change the topic?"

"You have spaghetti sauce all over your chin," Cole pointed out.

I made a face at him. "Very helpful," I muttered. "Guess I've been sitting across the table from *you* for too long. I'm picking up your habits."

34

He stuck out his tongue at me. He had half a meatball on his tongue. Very mature.

"I forgot to ask you about basketball practice yesterday," Dad chimed in. "How did that —"

"Bad topic!" I interrupted.

Mom set down her fork. She blew a strand of hair off her forehead. "Guess every topic is a bad one tonight, huh?"

"Maybe," I grumbled, lowering my eyes to my plate. I shook my head. "I was terrible at practice. Coach Clay gave me a chance, and I played like a perfect klutz."

"No one's perfect," Cole chimed in.

"Cole, be quiet," Mom scolded.

"Doesn't anyone want to hear about my sprained thumb?" Cole whined.

"No," Mom shot back. "Be quiet." She turned back to me. "You didn't play well?"

"I — I tripped over my own dribble. Twice," I stammered. "And I missed an easy layup. The ball didn't even touch the rim."

"Well . . . next time . . ." Dad started.

"But this was my big chance to show I can be a starter!" I cried. "And I blew it. I just felt so tired. I hadn't slept the night before. And . . . and . . ."

"You're still the sixth player," Mom said soothingly. "You'll get a chance."

"Do you have team practice tomorrow?" Dad asked, helping himself to more salad.

I shook my head. "No. Tomorrow afternoon is chorus practice. Cole has it, too. You know. The chorus is performing for the junior high graduation next month."

"I get to sing two solos," Cole bragged. "I'm the only fifth grader in the chorus — and I'm the only one with perfect pitch."

"No one's perfect," I reminded him. I know. It was a really lame joke. No one laughed.

Mom lowered her eyes to Cole's hand. "How did you sprain your thumb?" she asked.

"I didn't," Cole replied. "I was just trying to get into the conversation."

Mrs. Mellon, the music teacher, was a tiny, birdlike woman. She always wore gray sweaters and gray skirts or pants. With her feathery gray hair and snipped beak of a nose, she always reminded me of a sparrow. Or maybe a chirping chickadee.

She called us her canaries.

Greene County Middle School wasn't big enough to have a music room. So the chorus met after school in a corner of the auditorium stage.

There were eight kids in the chorus. Four boys and four girls. Mostly sixth graders, with a few younger kids like Cole thrown in. It was hard to put a chorus together in such a small school.

Mrs. Mellon was late. So the boys shot paper

clips across the stage at each other with rubber bands. And the girls talked about how dumb the boys were.

When Mrs. Mellon finally arrived, her hands fluttering tensely at her feathery hair, she wanted to get right down to business. "Our performance is two weeks from tonight," she announced fretfully. "And we really don't know what we're doing — do we?"

We all pretty much agreed that we needed a lot more rehearsal time. Lucy-Ann, who is our only soprano, raised her hand. "Maybe we could lip-synch some songs," she suggested. "You know. From records."

Everyone laughed.

I studied Lucy-Ann. I wasn't so sure she was joking.

"No fooling around this afternoon," Mrs. Mellon said sternly. "Let's see how much we can get done when we're being serious."

We sang our warm-up scales. We were interrupted when a large black spider dropped from the rafters into Lucy-Ann's curly blond hair. She shrieked and staggered back. And she began shaking her head wildly and tugging at her curls with both hands.

Finally, the spider dropped onto the stage floor, and Cole tromped on it.

"Isn't that bad luck or something?" a boy named Larry called to my brother.

Cole shrugged and scraped the sole of his shoe against the floor.

"Let's begin with 'Beautiful Ohio,'" Mrs. Mellon suggested, ignoring the whole spider problem. She shuffled sheet music on her music stand. "That's the one that gave us so much trouble last time."

"It's the high part that's the problem," Lucy-Ann chimed in.

"It's your *voice* that's the problem!" Larry teased Lucy-Ann. I think he has a crush on her. He's always insulting her.

Mrs. Mellon cleared her throat. "Please, folks. Serious. Serious." She turned to Cole. "Have you been practicing your solo?"

"Oh, yeah. Sure," my brother lied.

"Then let's try it," Mrs. Mellon suggested. "Remember, Cole — you wait *three* beats before you come in."

"No problem," Cole told her.

At the last rehearsal, he didn't do it right *once*.

Mrs. Mellon raised her arms. Smiled. And fluttered her hands, her signal for us to start.

We began to sing "Beautiful Ohio." It's kind of a drippy song, but I like to sing the high part.

"Very good. Very good," Mrs. Mellon encouraged us as we sang, a tight smile on her face.

It *did* sound pretty good.

Until Cole began his solo.

I saw him take a deep breath. He stepped forward. Waited for three beats. Opened his mouth.

And sang: "BLUCK BUCK BUCK BLUU-UCK BLUCK."

"Huh?" Mrs. Mellon gasped.

We all stopped singing. I stared hard at my brother.

He had a confused expression on his face. He kept clearing his throat.

"Sing the words, Cole," Mrs. Mellon instructed sternly. "You *do* know the words — right?"

Cole nodded.

"Let's begin with the chorus just before Cole's solo," she told us.

We began again. As I sang, I kept my eyes on my brother.

I saw him count off the three beats. Then:

"BLUCK BLUCK BLUCK CLUCK BUCK!"

What was he trying to prove?

Larry laughed. But no one else did.

Cole kept rubbing his neck and clearing his throat. His face was bright red.

"*Are you okay?*" I mouthed the words to him.

He didn't answer me.

"Cole — please!" Mrs. Mellon pleaded. "Stop fooling around. We really haven't time." She frowned at him. "You have a beautiful voice. I know you can sing this. Will you please do your part?"

She raised her hands. "Begin on three," she told him. "One . . . two . . . three . . ." She began conducting with one hand. "Now let's hear your best," she urged.

"BLUCK BLUCK BUCK BUCK BUCK!" my brother clucked in a high, silly voice.

I stepped away from the other girls and rushed up to him. "Cole — what is the big idea?" I cried furiously. "Why are you doing that?"

"BLUCK BLUCK BUCK CLUCK BLUCK," he replied.

Later, I was up in my room, wrapping Lucy-Ann's birthday present. I glanced to the doorway and saw Cole standing there tensely.

His blond hair stood up straight on top of his head. He was wiping his sweaty hands on the front of his T-shirt.

"What do you want?" I asked sharply. "I'm busy." I folded a corner of the birthday wrapping paper and taped it down over the CD case.

Cole cleared his throat, but didn't reply.

I shook my head at him. "You ruined the whole rehearsal," I told him.

"It wasn't my fault!" he cried shrilly.

"Hah!" I slammed my scissors down on the desk. "You refused to sing. You stood there clucking like a hen! Whose fault *was* it?"

"You don't understand —" Cole croaked, tenderly rubbing his throat.

"No, I don't," I interrupted angrily. "You know, we're all tired of your dumb jokes. Especially me.

You just think you're so funny all the time, Cole. But you're really such a pain."

"But I wasn't being funny!" he protested, stepping into the room. He walked up to the desk and fiddled nervously with the tape dispenser. "I didn't want to cluck like that. I — I couldn't help it."

I rolled my eyes. "For sure," I muttered.

"No — really, Crystal. I — I think Vanessa made me do it! I think she made me cluck like that!"

I laughed. "I'm not stupid, you know," I told him. "I may fall for the same joke of yours once or twice. But I'm not going to fall for it again."

"But Crystal —"

"It wasn't funny," I repeated. "And it wasn't fair for you to ruin the whole rehearsal for everyone."

"You don't understand!" Cole protested. "It wasn't a joke. I really *had* to cluck. I —"

"Out!" I shouted. I made shooing motions with both hands. "Out of my room — now!"

His face turned bright red. He started to say something. Changed his mind with a defeated sigh. Turned and slumped out of my room.

"Anything for a joke, huh, Cole?" I murmured to myself.

I'm usually not that mean to my brother. But this time he deserved to be taught a lesson.

I finished wrapping the present. Then I did homework until bedtime.

I turned out the light and was climbing between the sheets when I heard a chicken clucking.

That's weird, I thought. I never hear the chickens at night. They're all locked in their coop.

"Cluuuuck bluuuuuck."

Sitting up, I stared across the dark room to the open window. My curtains fluttered in a soft breeze. A triangle of pale moonlight slanted over the carpet.

Did the chicken coop door come open? I wondered.

Did a chicken escape somehow?

"Bluuck bluuck buuck."

The cry seemed to be coming from close to the house, beneath my bedroom window.

Watching the fluttering curtains, I climbed out of bed and crossed the room to the window. The moonlight washed over me, cold and silvery.

"Bluck bluck cluck."

I leaned on the window ledge. Peered down to the ground.

And gasped.

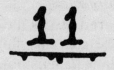

11

Nothing down there.

No chicken.

I stared at the silvery ground. Then moved my eyes to the long chicken coop beside the garage. It sort of looked like a long, low, wooden doghouse. The door was shut tight. Nothing moved inside its tiny round windows.

"Bluuuuck bluuuck."

Feeling confused, I pulled my head inside. Where was that clucking coming from?

From inside?

"Cluuck cluuuck."

Yes. I could hear it through the wall. The wall to my brother's room next door.

Why is he doing that? I asked myself, climbing back into bed. Why is he in there clucking in the middle of the night?

What is he trying to prove?

* * *

I knew Lucy-Ann's birthday party would be fun. Lucy-Ann always throws great parties.

She comes from a big farm family. She has seven brothers and sisters.

Their big farmhouse is always filled with great smells — chickens roasting, pies baking. Lucy-Ann's parents are the most successful farmers in Goshen Falls. And they're really nice people, too.

Lucy-Ann invited the whole class to her party, and about two dozen of her relatives. It was a beautiful spring afternoon. And a lot of people were already hanging out in the yard in front of the tall, white farmhouse when I arrived.

Lucy-Ann has a lot of little cousins. As I hurried up the gravel drive, I saw a bunch of them hanging around the side of the utility barn. Lucy-Ann's dad was giving tractor rides, and the little kids were jumping up and down, wrestling each other in excitement, waiting their turns.

I met Lucy-Ann at the top of the drive and handed her the wrapped-up CD.

She studied the square-shaped box and grinned. "Wow. I'll *never* guess what this is!" she joked.

"Okay, okay. So I'm not too original," I replied with a shrug.

"You don't know what a perfect present it is," she said as we began to walk across the grass to the others. "Mom and Dad got me a Discman for my birthday — but no CDs."

I laughed. "Well, now you've got *one*," I said. "At least I know you don't already have it!"

Lucy-Ann's expression turned serious. "Are you going to chorus rehearsal tomorrow morning?"

I nodded. "Yeah. We really need to practice."

"I'll be a little late," Lucy-Ann said. "We usually don't get back from church till after eleven-thirty." She frowned. "Did you talk to your brother? Why did he act like such a total jerk yesterday? What was all that horrible clucking? Did he think it was funny or something?"

I shrugged. "Yeah. I guess." Then I added with a sigh, "No way I can explain my brother. Sometimes I think he's from Mars."

Lucy-Ann laughed. "Tell me about it," she muttered. "I've got *four* brothers!"

I waved to a couple of girls from my class who were leaning against the broad trunk of an old maple tree. I walked over to talk to them.

I like a lot of kids in my class, although I don't get to see some of them outside of school. You see, Goshen Falls is so tiny, and we have the only middle school for miles. So kids are bussed to our school from all over the county.

That means some of my friends live over thirty miles away. When I want to call them at night, it's a long-distance call!

It was a nice party. We stayed outside the whole time. Lucy-Ann cranked up the volume on her tape player, and we all danced. I mean, all the girls danced. A couple of the boys joined in. But most of them stood on the grass, making jokes about those who were dancing.

I really had fun — until birthday cake time.

And then the fun turned to horror.

12

As the afternoon sun started to lower itself behind the farmhouse, Lucy-Ann's mom carried out the birthday cake. Actually, she carried out *two* cakes — one vanilla from the bakery and one chocolate that she baked herself.

"With so many kids in our family," Lucy-Ann explained to me, "no one could ever decide what kind of cake everyone liked best. So Mom always has to bake an extra for every birthday!"

We all grabbed plates and gathered around the long, white-tableclothed table to sing "Happy Birthday" to Lucy-Ann. Beside the two cakes stood a blueberry pie about the size of a pizza!

It took a long while to light the candles on both cakes. The wind kept gusting and blowing some of the candles out.

Finally, Lucy-Ann's parents got them all lighted, and we sang "Happy Birthday." Lucy-Ann looked really pretty standing behind the cakes, the flickering candlelight dancing over her face and curly blond hair.

She seemed to be staring at me as we sang.

And I suddenly realized that something was wrong.

That loud clicking sound I heard — it was coming from me!

My lips were clicking together noisily as I sang.

As soon as the song ended, I rubbed my lips with my finger. They felt very dry. Sort of cracked and dry.

"Crystal — what kind of cake?" Lucy-Ann was asking. I gazed up to see her and her mother slicing the cakes.

I held my plate up. "A little bit of both?" I couldn't decide, either.

Balancing my plate and fork in one hand, I walked off to join some friends. "Looks good," I said.

I mean, I tried to say it. But it came out, *"Tc-ccck tccccck."* Sort of a metal click.

I ran my tongue over my lips. So dry.

"Tcccck tcccccck."

I tried to chew a forkful of cake. But each bite made that loud clicking sound.

I licked my lips again.

Tried to chew.

I started to choke. I couldn't chew the cake.

49

"Ckkkkkkk tccccck."

A few kids were staring at me.

"Crystal, are you okay?" someone asked.

I clicked a reply. Then I hurried to Lucy-Ann at the table. "Do you have any Chap Stick?" I demanded shrilly.

My lips clicked as I talked. She struggled to understand me.

"Chap Stick?" I repeated. *"Chpsttttccck?"*

She nodded, narrowing her eyes to study me. "In the medicine chest. Downstairs bathroom on the left." She pointed.

I set down my cake plate and took off, running across the grass. I pulled open the screen door and flew into the house. It smelled sweet inside, from all the cake and pie baking.

I turned to the left, into the hallway. I knew my way. I'd spent a lot of hours with Lucy-Ann here.

The bathroom door stood open. I stepped inside, clicked on the light, and shut the door behind me.

Then I dove to the medicine cabinet and gazed into the mirror.

It took my eyes a few seconds to adjust. But when I could finally focus on my lips — I opened my mouth in a shrill scream of horror.

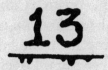

13

Bright red, my lips poked out from my face.

I ran a finger across them. Both lips were bumpy. Hard and bumpy.

I tapped my lips with my finger. It made a soft *click*.

My lips were *hard*. They didn't feel like skin anymore! They felt as hard as fingernails!

"*Tcccck tcccck.*"

I clicked them. Opened and closed my mouth. Staring hard at the ugly reflection in the mirror.

Had my lips grown some sort of crust? Were my real lips underneath?

I raised both hands and struggled to pull the crusty part off.

But no. No crust. The hard lips were attached to my face.

"Oww!" I gasped. My lips clicked shut.

"What is *happening* to me? It — it's like a *bird* beak! I can't let anyone see me like this!" I cried out loud.

51

I banged the mirror with both fists. This *can't* be happening! I told myself in a complete panic. It *can't*!

I tried to pull the hard beak lips off one more time.

"Crystal — calm down. Calm down!" I instructed myself. I took a deep breath and forced myself to turn away from the mirror.

It's an allergic reaction, I decided.

That's all. I ate something I am allergic to.

It will disappear in a few hours. And if it doesn't disappear, Dr. Macy will know how to shrink the lips back to normal and make them soft again.

I took another deep breath. My whole body was shaking. I was trembling so hard, my lips were clicking.

I shut my eyes. Then I turned back to the mirror. I opened them, praying my real lips would be back.

But no.

"A bird beak," I murmured in a shaky whisper. "It looks like a bird beak."

Click click.

I ran my tongue over the bumpy lips.

Ow. The hard lips scratched my tongue.

I can't let anyone see me like this! I decided. I'll sneak out the front door and run home. I'll explain to Lucy-Ann later.

I shut off the light and pulled the bathroom door open a crack. No one in the house, I saw.

Everyone was still out in the back, enjoying the cakes and pie.

Will I ever enjoy cake again? I wondered.

Or will I have to pull up worms from the ground and suck them through my bird lips?

Sickening thoughts.

I crept along the living room. Then pushed open the front door — and escaped.

As I ran to the road, I could hear the happy voices from behind the house. Kids were laughing and shouting over the boom of dance music.

I turned and started running full speed toward home. I hoped no one could see me.

The sun had sunk behind the trees. Evening shadows reached across the ground toward me.

My lips clicked as I ran. My heart pounded. I ran all the way home without slowing down once. Luckily, I didn't run into anyone I knew on the street.

Mom and Dad's car was gone. I ran up the driveway and into the house through the kitchen door.

Cole turned shakily from the sink. "Crystal —!" he cried. I could tell instantly that something was wrong.

I turned my face away. I didn't want him to see my ugly bird mouth.

But he rushed forward, grabbed my arm, and turned me around. "Mom and Dad aren't home," he murmured. "I — I have to show you something."

"Cole — what is it?" I demanded, my lips clicking. "Why are you — *click click* — wearing that bath towel around your neck?"

"I . . . need help," he replied, lowering his eyes.

He slowly unwrapped the blue bath towel. Then he slid it off his neck. "Look," he insisted.

I gasped.

Feathers!

He had white feathers poking out from his neck and shoulders.

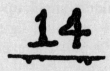

14

"Cole — when did this happen?" I shrieked.

"BLUCCCK BLUUUCK BUCCCCK," he clucked, his eyes wide with horror.

"Stop it!" I cried angrily. "This is no time for your stupid clucking!"

And then I realized that he had tricked me again. The feathers weren't really growing from his body. He had glued them on or something.

"BLUUUCK. I . . . can't . . . stop the clucking!" he choked out, rubbing his throat.

"Yeah. Sure," I replied, rolling my eyes. I reached out and plucked a white feather from the back of his neck.

I expected the fake feather to slide off easily.

But my brother's hands shot up. "OUCH!" he screamed.

The tip of the feather left a small hole in his skin. I grabbed a big feather on his shoulder — and pulled it.

"Hey — careful!" Cole cried, moving away

from me. "BLUUUCK CLUUUCK. That really hurts!"

"Oh, no!" I gasped. "They're real! You ... you're really growing — *click click* — feathers!"

"Uh ... uh ... uh ..." Cole started to whimper. His feathery shoulders shook up and down.

"Take it easy," I told him. I guided him gently into his room. "I'll pull them off. I'll be really careful. You'll be okay."

I made him sit down on the edge of the bed. I leaned over him and started to pluck out the white feathers. I tried to be as gentle as I could. But he jumped each time I tugged one out.

"We've got to tell Mom and Dad," he said softly, his eyes lowered to the floor. "Ouch."

"They're almost all out," I told him. I plucked a long one off the back of his neck. He jumped. "No problem. You will look perfectly normal."

"But we've still got to tell Mom and Dad," he insisted.

"Do you think they'll believe us?" I asked. My hard lips clicked with each word.

Cole gazed up at me. "Hey — what's up with your lips?"

"Oh — I — uh ..." I covered them with one hand. "Just chapped," I said. "Very chapped."

I don't know why. I didn't want to let him know that weird things were happening to me, too.

"You look disgusting!" Cole exclaimed. "Yuck!"

It seemed to cheer him up a lot.

I tugged the last two feathers out as hard as I could.

"Hey — !" he cried out angrily. He rubbed a hand over the back of his neck.

I stepped back. White feathers covered the bed and floor. "You'd better pick them up," I clicked.

He clucked in reply.

I still had one hand over my mouth. I didn't need any more comments from him about how disgusting my lips looked. I hurried to the bathroom to find some cream for them.

Mom and Dad stayed out very late. Cole and I tried to stay awake because we wanted to talk to them. But finally, we gave up and went to bed.

Sunday morning I woke up late. The sun was already high in the sky. Orange sunlight washed over my room from the open window. A soft breeze ruffled my feathers.

Huh? Feathers?

"Ohhhh." I sat up with a groan. My neck itched like crazy. My arms itched, too.

I blinked myself awake. And stared at the white feathers up and down my arms.

I opened my mouth to scream. But all that came out was a choked *"goggle goggle goggle."* Like a clucking hen.

I leaped out of bed and hurtled to the dresser mirror. I pulled down the top of my nightshirt and gasped. My shoulders and arms were covered with fluffy, white and brown feathers.

I brushed my hand over my lips. They had grown even harder. Hard as bone.

I saw something move in the mirror. I twirled around to find Cole in my bedroom doorway.

"Crystal —" he clucked. He staggered into the room. White feathers bristled on his shoulders and under his chin. They had grown back.

"Look at me!" I clicked.

"BLUCCK BLUCCCCK," Cole replied.

I turned back to the mirror and started frantically pulling off my feathers. It hurt each time. But I didn't care. I wanted them *off!*

It didn't take long. I plucked them all off. Then I gathered them up and tossed them into the wastebasket. Then I helped Cole remove his feathers.

His lips had hardened during the night. His fingernails had grown. His hands suddenly looked sort of like claws.

"Vanessa," he murmured.

I stared at him. I knew instantly what he meant.

I had been thinking the same thing all along. Remembering the horrible moment we spilled Vanessa's groceries.

"Yes," I agreed. "I didn't want to admit it. I didn't want to believe it. But Vanessa did this to us. Vanessa is BLUUUUCCK BLUCCCK turning us into chickens."

"Chicken chicken," he clucked.

I heard clattering sounds downstairs in the kitchen. Mom and Dad!

"We have to BLUUUUCK tell them!" I cried. "We have to tell them everything!"

Cole and I both bolted for the bedroom door at the same time. We squeezed through together. Then we ran side by side down the hall.

I could hear Mom's voice from the kitchen.

Cole and I started calling to her as we hurried down the stairs.

"Mom — we need BLUUUCCK help!" I cried. "It's Vanessa. She really *does* have BLUUUCCK CLUUCK powers!"

"She's turning us into chickens!" Cole called to Mom as we reached the downstairs hall and went running to the kitchen. "We're growing feathers and everything!"

"It's the truth!" I cried. "You've got to help us. Cole and I — BLUUUCK — we're both turning into chickens!"

"That's good news," Mom replied calmly. "I need two more chickens for the barbecue this afternoon."

15

"Huh?"

"Barbecue us?"

Cole and I both gasped. Was Mom joking?

As soon as we burst into the kitchen, I realized that Mom wasn't talking to us. She was on the phone. She had her back to us and was drumming her fingernails on the Formica counter beside the phone.

My eyes swept over the kitchen. It was cluttered with pans and serving bowls, cut-up lettuce and tomatoes, a bag of potatoes, bottles of barbecue sauce, and a pile of chicken parts on a tray beside the sink.

What a mess!

"Mom — we . . . we CLUUUCK BLUUUCK have to talk to you!" I sputtered.

She turned, still talking, and waved. She said a few more words, then hung up the phone. "You two slept so late," she said, frowning at the wall clock. "It's nearly noon, and our guests will be here in an hour or two."

"Mom —" I started.

She wiped her forehead with the back of her hand and moved toward the sink. "Did you forget we're having a big barbecue this afternoon? We're having at least twenty guests, and — and —" She gestured to the pile of chicken parts.

The sight of them made my stomach turn.

"Cluuucck bluuuck," Cole murmured.

I stepped over to the sink. "We have to talk to you," I said, taking Mom's arm. "Cole and I — we have a problem. A real problem."

"About the chorus practice you missed this morning?" Mom interrupted. She took a small brush and began slapping barbecue sauce on the chicken parts. Then she tossed each part in a big china bowl.

"No, Mom. I —"

"That was Mrs. Mellon on the phone," Mom continued. "She wondered where you were. She was calling to make sure you two were okay."

"We're *not* okay," I said solemnly.

"She's such a nice woman. She's bringing two barbecued chickens of her own this afternoon. For people who don't like them hot and spicy the way I make them."

She turned to me. "Crystal, you can help me cut up the peppers."

"Mom — please!" Cole cried. "Stop talking about the chickens!"

"We have something to tell you," I said.

"Your dad is out back, getting the barbecue grills ready," Mom said, brushing red sauce on a wing. "Oh! Ice! We have to remember to buy ice!"

"Mom — Cole and I are turning into chickens," I told her.

She laughed. "Ice and paper plates," she murmured. "I don't want to use real plates. Too much of a mess."

"No. Really!" I grabbed her arm. The brush fell into the chicken bowl.

"Crystal — I really don't have time," Mom sighed. She blew a strand of hair off her forehead and picked up the brush. "You and Cole should get yourself some breakfast — or lunch. Then see if you can help your dad."

"BLUUUUCK!" Cole exclaimed.

"Listen to me, Mom," I begged. "Do you hear Cole clucking like that?"

"Yes. Very nice clucking," she murmured, tossing a leg into the bowl.

"Do you see my lips?" I demanded. "Vanessa is doing this to us. We bumped Vanessa and spilled her groceries. So she is turning us CLUUUUCK into chickens."

"Please, you two," Mom groaned. "Can't you see how frantic I am? I don't have time to —"

She stopped when she glimpsed my lips. "Yuck! Those are really chapped."

"They're not chapped!" I screamed. "I'm growing a beak!"

"CLUUUCK BLUUUCK," Cole added.

Mom tossed up her hands. "Go put some cream on your lips, Crystal. And keep out of my way, okay? I don't have time for jokes today. If you're not going to help, just don't make more trouble."

I turned to Cole. He shook his head unhappily.

We both slumped out of the room. "Do you think Dad will listen to us?" Cole asked weakly.

I clicked my lips. "I don't think so," I muttered. "He's as busy as Mom is."

"Then what can we do?" Cole asked. He scratched his neck. Were the feathers growing back already?

An idea popped into my head. "Anthony!" I cried.

"Huh? What about him?" Cole demanded.

"Anthony was with us!" I explained. "The same thing is probably happening to him. He's probably changing into a chicken like us."

Cole rubbed his chin hard. "Cluuuuck. Bluuuuck. Yeah. Probably."

"So if *all three* of us tell our story to Mom and Dad, then maybe they'll believe us!" I cried.

"It's worth a try," Cole agreed excitedly. "Let's hurry over to Anthony's house."

We each grabbed a glass of orange juice. And a Pop-Tart, which we ate raw.

Then we ran out the front door and headed to Anthony's house.

We had run less than a block when we bumped into Vanessa.

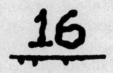

16

Well. This time we didn't really bump into her.

I saw her before Cole did, hurrying toward us on the other side of the street. Despite the heat, she was dressed all in black. She wore a black cotton shawl over the shoulders of her black dress. It fluttered behind her as she strode along the sidewalk.

"Oh — it's *her!*" Cole whispered, poking me in the side.

We both stopped in the middle of the sidewalk and stared openmouthed as she approached.

Would she say something to us?

Could I work up the nerve to say something to her?

My heart pounded. My lips clicked nervously.

Cole's head started bobbing up and down on his neck. Just like a chicken. He let out a frightened cluck.

My poor brother.

Seeing him like that made me forget my fear. "Vanessa — !" I shouted.

She kept walking, taking those long, gliding strides of hers. Her shawl fluttered behind her.

"Vanessa —!" I repeated her name.

She had a look of solemn concentration on her face. I don't think she had even seen Cole and me.

Finally, she stopped. She stared across the street at us as if she didn't recognize us.

"BLUUUUCK BLUUUCK!" my brother clucked angrily.

That brought a smile to her black-lipsticked lips. She laughed, and her dark eyes flashed.

She brushed back her straight, black hair. "Bluck bluck to you, too!" she called. "Chicken chicken!" Then she turned and hurried along the sidewalk.

"Bluuuck — wait!" Cole called after her. His head bobbed frantically up and down.

"You have to *help* us!" I cried, my hard lips clicking.

Vanessa began walking faster. Her black hair flew behind her. She didn't look back.

We found Anthony fiddling around with a golf club in his front yard. He had borrowed one of his dad's putters. And he had scooped out a hole in the middle of the grass.

We watched him sink a long putt as we ran

across the front lawn. He flashed us two thumbs up. "Awesome, huh? I've been practicing."

"Awesome," I muttered. I was still thinking about Vanessa, still feeling really upset and frightened.

"Bluuck buuck," Cole said.

Anthony narrowed his eyes at him. "What's up, guys? My parents are going to your barbecue. But I have soccer practice."

Anthony pulled the ball from the hole and carried it a few feet away. He set it down, then leaned over the putter and prepared to putt again.

"Anthony, has anything weird been happening to you?" I blurted out.

"Yeah," Cole chimed in. "In the last two days — anything really weird?"

Anthony swung the golf club. It made a solid *thwock* as the club hit the ball. The ball sailed across the grass and stopped a few inches from the hole.

Anthony raised his eyes to us. "Yeah," he replied. "Something weird *has* been happening. How did you know?"

"Because BLUUUCK the same weird thing has been happening to us," I told him.

He stared hard at me. "Huh?"

Cole and I nodded.

Anthony made a face. He pretended to study

67

his golf club. "You mean you suddenly started putting really well, too?" he asked.

It was our turn to be surprised. "Putting? What does putting have to do with it?" I cried.

"Well, that's what's so weird," Anthony replied. "Before this weekend, I was a lousy putter. Really bad news. I couldn't even play minigolf!"

"So what?" Cole chimed in.

"So this weekend I'm really good at it," Anthony continued. He twirled the club in his hand. "All of a sudden, I'm not a bad putter. Don't you think that's weird?"

"But — but — but —" I sputtered.

"What about growing feathers?" Cole demanded. "And what about your lips?"

Anthony's face filled with confusion. Then he turned to me. "What's with your brother? Is he going totally mental or what?"

"Are you clucking all the time?" Cole asked Anthony.

Anthony laughed. He cut it short quickly. "I don't get it. Is this a joke or something, guys?"

I pulled my brother to the driveway. "He doesn't know what we're talking about," I whispered. "For some reason, it isn't happening to him."

Cole's head bobbed up and down. He let out a low cluck.

"Let's go," I said. "Anthony isn't going to be any help."

"I don't get the joke," Anthony repeated.

"See you BLUUUCK later!" I called to him. I started pulling Cole down the street. "We've got to help out with the barbecue."

"Maybe I can come after soccer practice," Anthony called. "Save me some chicken!"

"Yeah. Sure," I muttered unhappily.

Guests were already arriving for the barbecue. I recognized my aunt Norma's red Honda in the driveway. And I saw the Walker family from down the block, heading around the side of the house to the back.

I ducked in through the front door and ran up to my room. I wanted to tell Mom what was happening to Cole and me. But I knew she was too busy. She wouldn't listen.

I closed the bedroom door carefully behind me. I didn't want anyone to see me until I checked myself out.

Sure enough, I found white and brown feathers sticking out from my neck and shoulders.

The feathers had just poked through the skin. So it was really hard to pull them out. I had to use tweezers for the smaller ones.

Pluck.

Pluck.

Pluck. . . .

Ow. Did that hurt!

I heard voices from down in the backyard. And through my bedroom window, I could see swirling smoke from the barbecue grills.

Ugh. I had always loved the aroma of barbecuing chicken. But now it sickened me. I felt my stomach lurch. I gagged. I held my hand over my mouth — my beak! — and waited for the nausea to fade.

I'll stay up in my room, I decided. I won't go downstairs.

But then I heard Mom calling me from the kitchen.

"Com-ing!" I yelled. I had no choice. I had to go down there.

I crossed my fingers on both hands. My fingers suddenly felt so bony, so scraggly. My nails were long and pointed. Maybe no one will notice what is happening to me, I prayed.

I made my way slowly downstairs to the kitchen. Mom had her hair tied up in a bun. She wore a long white apron, covered with barbecue sauce stains.

She was mixing a big bowl of salad. But she stopped when I slipped into the room. "Crystal, where have you been? Guests are arriving. I need you to go out and be a hostess while I finish up in here."

"Okay, Mom. No problem," I replied. I let out a couple of soft clucks.

"See if there is enough ice," Mom instructed. "And tell your dad he may need more charcoal. We —"

She stopped suddenly, with a gasp.

She stared out the window. "Crystal — what on earth is your brother doing out there?"

I stepped up beside her and gazed out the window. "Oh, no!" I cried.

I couldn't *believe* what I saw.

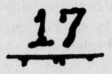

17

Cole had climbed into the area fenced off for the chickens. He was down on his elbows and knees. There were chickens all around him.

"What is he *doing?*" Mom repeated, raising a hand to one cheek.

I knew what he was doing. But I knew this wasn't the time to tell Mom. Not with twenty guests waiting for their dinner.

I peered out the window. Cole was pecking seeds off the ground.

I watched him lower his head to the gravel. I watched his lips open and his tongue slide out. I watched him suck up some chicken feed. His head bobbed up as he swallowed it down.

"Why is your brother acting so dumb in front of company?" Mom asked, shaking her head. "Does he think that's *funny?*"

"I don't know, Mom," I replied. Cole's head lowered, and he sucked up more seed from the gravel.

People were laughing at him. Some just stared in confusion.

"Well, go out there and stop him," Mom ordered, turning back to the salad bowl. "Pull him away from the chickens and drag him into the house, Crystal. I want an explanation from him."

"Okay, Mom," I murmured.

I watched Cole pecking at seeds for a few seconds more. Then I made my way out the kitchen door and crossed the yard to the chicken area.

"Cole?" I called softly. I stepped over the wire fence. "Cluuuck Cluuuck Cole?"

I really did plan to bring him into the house to Mom.

I really did plan to drag him away from there.

But those seeds looked so delicious!

I bumped some chickens out of the way. Then I dropped down on my knees, lowered my head — and started pecking away.

The next day in school, I don't think I heard a word anyone said. I couldn't stop thinking about the barbecue.

Of course, all of our guests thought what Cole and I did was some kind of a joke. They didn't *get* the joke. But they knew it had to be a joke.

Mom and Dad were really angry. They needed us to help out. But we were too busy pecking seeds with the chickens.

Later, Mom was really upset when Cole and I

refused to eat any of her barbecued chicken. "It was always your favorite!" she cried.

Not anymore, I thought sadly.

The idea of eating a chicken made my insides feel as if they were turning inside out!

The next morning, I needed Cole's help in pulling all the feathers from my neck and shoulders. Some big white feathers had poked out of my back, and I couldn't reach them.

It took us each twenty minutes to pluck out all the feathers that had grown during the night. We hid them in my sweater drawer. We didn't want Mom or Dad to see them before we had a chance to explain.

The school day went so slowly. My neck and back kept itching. I prayed that feathers wouldn't grow while I was in school.

And I prayed that none of my teachers would call on me in class. I was clucking more and more. It was becoming a real struggle to talk.

My team had a basketball game in the gym after school against a girls' team from the next county. I had looked forward to it all week. But now I just wanted to hurry home before any kids saw me clucking or pecking seeds from the playground.

I dropped my books in my locker. And I was sneaking to the front door of the school — when Coach Clay turned the corner. "Crystal, I was *looking* for you!" she cried.

74

"Cluck?" I replied.

"Hilary has a bad cold. I'm going to let you start at forward today," she told me.

"Cluck —" I started.

But she didn't give me a chance to reply. She placed her hands on my shoulders, turned me around, and marched me to the locker room. "I know you're going to be great," she said. "Go get changed."

"Cluck," I told her. Normally, I'd be totally pumped! I was going to be the starting forward. This is what I had dreamed about all year!

As I changed into my uniform, the other girls all came over to slap me high fives and wish me good luck.

Maybe I can do it, I told myself. Maybe I will play really well. Maybe I *can* show them just how good a player I am.

But as soon as the game started, I knew I was in trouble.

Big trouble.

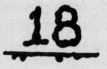

18

Our team won the opening jump. I turned and began running to the other team's basket.

I leaned forward as I ran. My head bobbed up and down.

Up and down. Up and down.

Low clucks escaped my throat.

I tried to straighten up. But I couldn't.

Our center took a shot. Missed. We all started to run back to the other basket.

"Nooooo," I moaned.

To my horror, I realized that I couldn't run without bobbing my head.

I glanced to the sideline — and saw Coach Clay staring at me. "Crystal — what are you *doing?*" she called.

I heard some kids laughing at me.

"Crystal — stop goofing," Gina, the other forward, scolded me.

The action moved to our opponents' basket, and I ran down court. My head bobbed up and down. I realized I was running stiff-legged. My knees no longer bent!

The ball came sailing toward me.

I couldn't catch it. My hands were tucked under my armpits. My elbows were poked out like wings.

I let out a loud cluck as the ball bounced off my shoulder.

My head bobbed up and down.

My teammates were yelling angrily at me. On the sideline, I saw Coach Clay shaking her head. Girls on the other team were laughing.

Down the court. I tried to pry my hands from my armpits as I ran. My head bobbed. My lips clicked.

I glanced down — and stopped.

No!

My legs.

White feathers were sprouting up and down my legs.

And everyone could see them.

I heard a whistle blow. The referee called a time out.

My teammates ran toward our bench. I took off in the other direction. I ran out of the gym and out of the school.

I wanted to run and run and never stop.

I hid in my room during dinner. I was so depressed — and frightened. I wanted to tell Mom and Dad everything. But what if they didn't believe me? What if they thought it was all a joke?

After dinner, Mom and Dad had to go to school for a Parents Association meeting. Cole and I waited until we heard the car pull away. Then we waddled downstairs to the living room.

We were down on our knees, pecking crumbs in the rug.

My body was covered with white and brown feathers. It would take hours to pull them all off.

"I — CLUUUUCK — I'm so scared," Cole stammered.

"Me, too," I confessed. I pecked at a big chunk of lint.

"Crystal, what are we going to do?" Cole asked softly.

I started to say, "I don't know."

But I suddenly knew exactly what we had to do.

19

We crept out into a cool, windy night. The swirling wind ruffled my feathers. Up above, a pale half-moon kept sliding behind wispy clouds.

Cole and I walked along the street that led to town. We tried to hurry. But our legs felt stiff, and our knees were hard to bend.

Car headlights swept over the street toward us. We slipped behind a low hedge and hid, clucking softly. We didn't want anyone to see us like this. And we didn't want anyone to ask us where we were going.

We passed through town, making our way along the backs of stores. Trees hissed and shook as the wind picked up. The air grew heavy and moist. I felt a few raindrops on my forehead.

A sweet aroma made me take a deep breath. It came from the bakery. I realized that Mrs. Wagner must be baking doughnuts for tomorrow morning.

A sad cry escaped my beak. Would I ever be

able to taste a doughnut again? Or would I spend the rest of my life pecking my food off the ground?

Cole and I turned onto the dirt path that led to Vanessa's old farmhouse. The night grew darker — and colder — as soon as we moved away from town.

Our shoes plodded heavily over the hard dirt path. A few minutes later, I could see the black outline of Vanessa's house against the gray sky.

"What are we CLUUUCK going to say to her?" Cole demanded softly.

I brushed a raindrop off my eyebrow. My hand felt rough and scratchy, my fingers hard as bone.

"I'm going to BLUUUCK tell her how sorry we are," I replied. "I'm going to tell her we didn't mean to knock over her groceries. That it was all a big accident. And we're sorry we didn't stay and help her pick them up. CLUUUUCK."

We stepped up to Vanessa's wooden fence. The gate had been left open. It banged in the wind.

I raised my eyes to the house. It hung over the tall grass like a low, dark creature. No lights on anywhere.

Had she already gone to sleep?

"I — I don't bluuuck think she's home," Cole whispered.

"Of course she's home," I replied sharply. "Where else would she cluuuuck be? There's nowhere to go at night in Goshen Falls."

We stepped through the gate. I tried to latch it behind us to stop it from banging. But the latch was broken.

"What do we say after we apologize?" Cole asked, hanging back.

I placed a hand on his shoulder and guided him along with me to the front door.

"Then we beg her to remove the spell," I clucked. "We beg her to change us back to the way we were."

"Do you think she'll do it?" he asked in a tiny voice.

"I don't know," I replied. "But we'll soon find out."

I knocked on the front door.

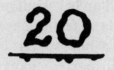

20

No answer.

The gate banged behind us. Startled, Cole and I both jumped.

I took a deep breath and pounded my scraggly fist on the door again.

We waited, staring straight ahead. Listening to the harsh whisper of the trees, and to the banging gate.

Silence in the house.

I uttered a sigh of disappointment and turned to my brother. "You were right. Vanessa isn't home."

We backed away from the house. Clouds floated away from the moon. The front window glinted with silvery moonlight.

"Let's peek inside," I urged.

We made our way to the window. Standing on tiptoes, we peered into the living room.

In the silvery light, I stared at the dark shapes of furniture. Old-fashioned, high-back chairs. A long couch covered with pillows. Bookshelves from floor to ceiling.

Everything was very old-looking. But I didn't see anything strange or frightening.

Then a stack of books caught my eye. They were piled on a small, square table beside the couch. The books were big and thick. And even in the pale light, I could see that their covers were old and cracked.

Squinting into the room, I spotted two more of them, lying open on the low coffee table in front of the couch.

"Cole —" I whispered, my heart starting to pound. "See those old books? Do you think they are books about magic?"

"Huh?" He pressed his face against the glass. "What do you mean?"

"You know. Bluuuck. Books about magic spells. Sorcery books. They look like they could be old spell books — don't they?"

He nodded. "Yeah. Maybe."

I plucked a white feather from under his chin.

"Owww!" he yelped. "Why'd you do that?"

I shrugged. "Sorry. It was bothering me." I turned my face back to the window and stared at the old books.

"Let's go," Cole urged, tugging my arm. "She isn't here."

"But those books are here," I replied, tugging myself free. "And if they *are* spell books, maybe we could find the right book. You know. Bluuu-uck. With the right spell. And we could change *ourselves* back to normal!"

Cole rolled his eyes. He clicked his beak. "Yeah. Sure. Then maybe I'll flap my arms and lay an egg!"

"Don't be sarcastic," I scolded him. "It may be a bad idea. But at least it's an idea."

I pulled him to the front door. I turned the knob — and pushed.

The heavy door creaked open.

"Bluuuuck. Let's just take a quick peek at those books," I told my brother, stepping into the cool darkness of the house. "What have we got to lose?"

I pulled Cole into the front hall. The house smelled of coffee and peppery spices. Sort of a sweet–sharp aroma.

I led the way into the living room. Silvery light flooded in through the front window.

The floorboards groaned beneath my shoes. I stopped beside the couch and stared at the pile of old books.

I reached out for the book on top of the stack — when a furious shriek made me stop.

"Ohhh!" I pulled my hand back.

"Vanessa —!" Cole cried.

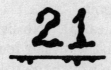

21

My breath caught in my chest. My heart skipped a beat.

I spun around — and saw Vanessa's cat leap onto the high back of an old armchair.

The cat's eyes flashed, golden in the pale light. It bared its teeth again in another angry hiss.

"I — I thought it was Vanessa," Cole murmured in a choked voice. "That cat cluuuuck doesn't want us here."

"Well, we're not staying long," I told the cat. I motioned for Cole to come over to the couch. "Help me check out these books. If we find the right one . . ."

As Cole passed by the chair, the cat swiped its claws at him.

"Hey —!" Cole ducked away from it.

"Cats don't like chickens," I whispered.

I picked up one of the open books on the coffee table. I raised it close to my face and tried to read the title in the dim light.

The print was smudged. The heavy cover was cracked with age and covered in a layer of dust. "I can't read it," I told Cole.

I saw him move to the wall. "I'll turn on a light," he suggested.

The cat hissed again.

"No — don't!" I called. "No light. If Vanessa comes back, we don't want her to see us."

I rubbed my finger over the title. And tried to focus on it.

"Hey — I don't believe it!" I cried happily.

"What is it, Crystal?" Cole called. "Did you find —"

Before I could answer, the ceiling light flashed on.

"Ohhh!" I cried out when I saw Vanessa standing by the wall.

22

I stumbled back.

The book dropped from my hand. It thudded heavily on the floor at my feet.

"Vanessa, I —"

I swallowed hard.

And realized I was staring at a painting. A huge oil portrait of Vanessa, hanging on the wall.

"Oh, wow!" I cried. "That painting — it's almost life-sized. I thought —"

I turned to Cole. He stood by the light switch, staring at the big portrait.

"Did *you* click on the light?" I demanded.

"Yes," he replied. "Sorry. I didn't mean to bluu-uck bluuuck scare you. I thought it would help you read the book title."

The book title!

"Cole — I think I found the right book!" I cried. "The very first book I picked up."

I bent down and excitedly lifted the old book from the floor.

Yes!

"Cole — look!" I exclaimed, holding up the front cover. "It's called *Chicken Chicken Chicken*. This has to be it! If I can find the spell that Vanessa used inside this book —"

"Then maybe we can reverse it!" Cole cried.

A loud *bang* from the front of the house made us both jump. The black cat screeched and jumped off the chair back. It scurried silently from the room.

"Was that the gate — or was it Vanessa?" I cried.

Cole clicked off the light. We listened, frozen in place. I gripped the old book closely to my chest.

Silence now. Then another bang. Just the fence gate in the wind.

"Let's get out of here," I whispered, raising my eyes to the front door.

"Bluuuuck," Cole replied. He turned and began walking stiff-legged to the door. Even in the dim light, I could see that a thick tuft of feathers had grown on the back of his neck.

Vanessa's cat stood on the hallway floor, arching its back as if ready to attack. We edged past it carefully.

"Nice kitty. Nice kitty," I murmured.

Its angry expression didn't change.

I pushed open the door. The gusting wind caught it and nearly blew the door handle out of my hand. Cole and I stepped outside. I tugged the door shut.

I carried the heavy book against my chest as we made our way home. We leaned into the wind. My hair fluttered up behind me like a pennant.

Goshen Falls stood in darkness. All of the stores close early. The only bright lights were at the self-serve gas station on the first corner.

Cole and I half-walked, half-trotted down the center of the street. I couldn't wait to get home and find the spell that Vanessa had used on us.

Finally, our house rose into view. The driveway was still empty. Mom and Dad hadn't returned yet from their meeting at school.

Good! I thought. Maybe I can find the spell and change Cole and me back to normal before they get home.

I led the way up the stairs to my room, still clutching the book to my chest. Cole closed the door behind us.

I dropped onto the edge of my bed and spread the big book on my lap. Cole stood beside me, clucking softly. Staring down at me as I rapidly flipped through the old pages, squinting hard at the tiny type.

"Well?" Cole demanded impatiently. "Is it in there? Is the spell in there?"

I didn't reply. I turned the pages furiously, my eyes running down each column. Faster. Faster. I turned page after page, my heart pounding.

"Well?" my brother demanded. "Well?"

I slammed the book shut in disgust.

"Noooooo!" I wailed. I tossed the book onto the bed.

"Cole," I cried, shaking my head sadly, "we've made a horrible mistake."

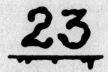

23

Cole uttered a squawk of horror. The white and brown feathers on the back of his neck stood up on end.

"Crystal — what's wrong?" he choked out.

"It's the wrong book!" I cried, jumping up from the bed. I left a pile of feathers where I'd been sitting. "It's a *cookbook!* It's a whole book of chicken recipes!"

"Yuck!" Cole cried.

The idea sent a wave of nausea up from my stomach. My arms suddenly itched. I gazed down and saw white feathers curling up from the skin.

"We have to go back there," I told my brother. My beak clicked loudly. It stretched out in front of my chin now. My teeth were sinking into my gums, about to disappear completely. I really had to struggle to form words.

Cole swallowed hard. "Go back?"

"Before it's too late," I whispered. "Before we're completely chicken — not human at all."

He gulped and didn't reply.

I hoisted up the book and started waddling to the bedroom door. I stopped in shock when I glimpsed my reflection in the dresser mirror.

My eyes! My head!

My eyes had changed into small, round circles. And the shape of my head was changing, too. Growing narrow. My eyes were far apart now, moving to the sides of my head.

"No! Oh, noooooo!" I opened my beak in a mournful wail.

"Come on — let's hurry!" Cole urged. He grabbed my hand. Feathers brushed feathers. The backs of our hands had sprouted a thick layer of short, white feathers.

"Yes. Hurry!" I repeated, bobbing my head up and down.

We made our way down the stairs and out the door. Back out into the dark, wind-swirled night.

I had a strong urge to bend down and peck some gravel from the driveway. But I fought it off and trotted to the street.

We had to hurry back there. Back to Vanessa's house.

Would we make it in time?

The trip was normally a ten-minute walk. But it took Cole and me much longer. Partly because our chicken legs were so stiff. And partly because it's a lot harder to see where you're going when your eyes are on different sides of your head!

The gusting winds softened a little as we finally reached Vanessa's farmhouse. Pale moonlight cast shadows over the broken shingled roof.

The windows were still dark. We leaned on the fence, catching our breath and studying the house. No sign that she had returned home.

Clutching the heavy recipe book to my chest, I pushed past the gate and led the way to the front door. Once again, it opened easily. Cole and I stepped inside, inhaling the strange, spicy fragrance of the house.

"Cluuuuck, Vanessa?" I called. "Hello? Anyone home?"

A pair of yellow eyes glared at us from the banister. The black cat let out a yawn. Not at all surprised to see us back. And from the way it stared at us, not at all pleased to have its home invaded once again.

"She isn't here," Cole whispered. "Let's bluuuck bluuuck hurry."

I dropped the recipe book on the coffee table and turned to the stack of books beside the couch. As I turned, a bowl on the coffee table caught my attention.

Sunflower seeds!

I couldn't resist. I poked my head into the bowl and began sucking the tasty seeds into my beak.

"Crystal — what are you *doing?*" Cole cried in a hoarse whisper. "Get away from there!"

He grabbed a book from the stack and began frantically pawing through it. I pecked up a few more seeds. Then I grabbed a book, too.

Cole let out a triumphant squawk. "These books — they're all magic books!" he declared.

"You're bluuuck right," I agreed. "Hundreds and hundreds of magic spells."

Cole flipped rapidly through the pages of his book. His eyes were practically spinning! "How will we ever find the right one?" he demanded.

"I think I just found it," I told him.

I carried the book to the window and held it up to the moonlight to see it better.

Yes!

"What does it say?" Cole asked excitedly. He dropped his book and came bobbing across the room to me.

"It's a whole cluuuuck page of chicken spells," I replied, holding the book up to the window. "This one is called 'Human into Chicken.' That sounds right — doesn't it?"

"No. Find 'Chicken into Human'!" Cole exclaimed.

My eyes swept over the pages. "No such thing," I told him. "We'll just have to reverse the 'Human into Chicken' spell."

"Well, go ahead!" he cried, his feathery head

bobbing up and down excitedly. "Reverse it! Do it! What do we have to do?"

I saw that he was so excited, he couldn't stand still. He tucked his hands under his armpits, stuck out his elbows to form wings — and began clucking round and round in a circle.

"Cole — bluuuck bluuck bluuuck!" I scolded.

He ignored me and kept clucking away. Flapping his arms and making a small circle over the floor.

I turned back to the book and carefully read the spell. It didn't look too hard. It didn't call for any special ingredients. It was just a bunch of words that had to be said rapidly. And the spell caster had to cluck a lot and do a simple dance.

Then, according to the book, you point at the poor victims and whisper, "Chicken chicken!"

Just as Vanessa had done to us.

"It looks pretty easy," I told Cole. "Stop dancing around, and I'll bluuuck try it."

He stopped his frantic flapping and circling. He turned to me. "Don't forget to cluuuck bluuck," he called.

I knew what he meant. He was reminding me to do the spell *backwards*.

Hmm . . . I glanced over the spell. That wasn't going to be so easy. But I had no choice. I had to try it.

Balancing the heavy, old book in one hand, I

pointed to Cole, then to myself, with my free hand. "Chicken chicken," I whispered.

Okay. That was the very end of the spell.

I lowered my eyes to the bottom of the page. And I started to read the words, going up: "Cluck cluck chick. Chick cluck cluck chick."

The spell instructed me to take three steps forward and two to the right. So I took two steps to the left, then three steps back.

I moved my scrawny chicken finger over the words, being careful to read them in reverse order:

"Chick cluck chick cluck. Cluck cluck chick."

Then, following the instructions backwards, I took two giant steps, then three steps to the right. I flapped my arms and clucked four times.

Then I read the *first* words of the spell at the top of the page: "Cluck cluck chick cluck. Cluck chick cluck."

That was it.

That was the whole spell. I had done it completely backwards.

Would it work? Would reversing Vanessa's spell turn Cole and me back to normal?

Would it do anything at all?

Yes.

Suddenly, I began to feel strange. My arms and legs began to itch like crazy. The feathers up and down my arms shot straight out.

The book fell from my hand and thudded loudly to the floor.

Egg-shaped spots sparkled in front of my eyes.

When the spots faded, the room turned purple and started to tilt.

"Hey — something is happening!" Cole cried in a tiny voice. He sounded far, far away.

Yes, something is happening, I agreed, grabbing the window ledge to keep from falling.

Something is happening.

But what?

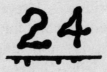

24

I felt so dizzy. The room rocked and swayed.

The floor suddenly appeared so far away. I blinked. Once. Twice.

The floor still seemed a mile below.

"Cluck cluck, Cole —?" I turned to my brother. Then I let out a shrill squawk of horror.

Now I knew why the floor seemed so far down. Cole and I had GROWN!

We weren't chickens anymore. We were BIIIIIG chickens!

"I — I'm as big as a *horse!*" I cried.

I gazed up. The ceiling was only an inch or two above my head.

Cole uttered a startled moan. His whole body trembled. Enormous feathers shook free and fell to the floor. He flapped his arms, and more feathers tumbled off him.

I saw Vanessa's black cat back into the hallway. Its yellow eyes were wide with fear. It arched its back and raised its tail and hissed at us furiously.

I took a step toward Cole. My big, feathery body bobbed in front of me. "I — I must have bluuuuuck done something wrong!" I told my brother.

Cole hopped up and down, bobbing his head. He clicked his beak, but no sound came out. Finally, he choked out, "Crystal — try again."

Yes. He was right. I had to try to reverse the spell again.

Maybe I couldn't turn us back into humans. But I might be able to shrink us back to our normal size.

I bent over to find the book on the floor. It was hard to find. I was so tall, the book looked about the size of a CD case!

It wasn't easy to pick it up, either. It kept sliding out from my scraggly chicken fingers.

It seemed like *hours* before I managed to find the spell again. Then I raised the little book up close to my right eye and began to perform the spell backwards once again.

Please, please, I prayed. *Let me get it right this time. Please, let Vanessa's spell reverse itself.*

I finished up with the final: "Cluck cluck chick cluck. Cluck chick cluck."

Would it work?

I heard Cole let out a choked cluck from across the room.

Once again, I began to feel weird. The egg-shaped spots sparkled in front of my eyes, blinding me with their brightness.

I shut my eyes.

I could feel the room tilting and swaying.

I tried to grab hold of something. But my hands grasped only air.

"Ooooh!" I let out a low moan as I felt myself start to fall. Yes. I was falling . . . falling . . .

When I opened my eyes, I didn't know where I was. The room had disappeared. I was surrounded by darkness. Surrounded by . . .

Whoa!

I gazed up at the book. The book of spells — it rested beside me on the floor. But it had grown! The book was taller than me!

"Cheep cheep!" I cried.

"Cheep cheep cheep," I heard Cole's tiny reply.

I spun around to find him. "Cheep?"

"Cheep cheep!"

He was a little yellow chick! I swallowed hard. I knew what that meant. That meant that I was *also* a tiny yellow chick!

I had reversed the spell — too much!

I struggled to speak — but I could only make a tiny *cheep cheep* sound. My tiny feet clicked on the wooden floor.

"Cheep cheep?" Cole asked. The poor little guy sounded so frightened.

My tiny heart was pounding in my feathery

yellow chest. I suddenly felt so angry. Why was this happening to us? Why did Vanessa think she had a right to do this to us?

I pecked my little beak furiously against the floor. I had no other way of letting out my anger.

But I didn't have much time to be angry.

A dark blur of motion made me raise my eyes.

I saw the giant shadow. No. It was Vanessa's cat. The cat perched on the desk next to an old-fashioned-looking typewriter.

Its tail smacked the typewriter as the cat dropped to the floor.

It crossed the room quickly, silently — and rose up over me, its eyes glowing with excitement.

It pulled back its lips, revealing its enormous teeth.

"Cheep cheep!" I squeaked. I froze in fear.

The cat pounced.

I felt its front paws wrap around my tiny, soft body.

Then the paws began to squeeze.

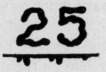

25

I tried to kick. I tried to thrash my arms. Tried to wriggle free.

But I was helpless against the giant cat.

Its big paws squeezed me until I could barely breathe.

Then it grabbed my head in its paws.

And lifted me — up. Up.

The cat dangled me in the air for a few seconds.

I wanted to scream.

I wanted to break free.

But I was helpless. Too weak and tiny to do anything.

The cat's eyes flashed as it dangled me in front of its face. Then it opened its mouth wide — and stuffed me inside.

Ohhhh. The cat's hot breath roared over me. The inside of its mouth felt so hot, so disgustingly sticky and wet.

"Cheep cheep cheeeep!" I squealed.

The cat bounced me around on its tongue.

And then — to my surprise — spit me out.

I fell hard onto my side on the floor. Behind me, I could hear Cole cheeping weakly.

I scrambled to my feet. I wanted to run.

But the cat grabbed me again. Lifted me high off the floor in its rough paws.

I saw the cat's head, tilted at an angle. I saw a gleam of silvery drool on its fangs. Felt its hot, sour breath roll over me once again.

The cat raised me high. Higher.

Is it going to swallow me this time? I wondered.

Is it going to shove me into its mouth and swallow me?

No. The purring creature let me drop back to the floor.

I landed on my back. My tiny feet clawed the air.

Before I could scramble to my feet, the cat picked me up again — this time by the foot. It swung me from side to side in front of its open mouth.

It's *playing* with me, I realized.

The cat is playing with its food!

And when it's finished playing . . . *then* it will eat me!

I could hear Cole cheeping down on the floor. The cat held me in one paw, dangling me in front of its face. Then it began batting me with its other paw, making me spin.

The spinning made me dizzy. I shut my eyes as the cat dropped me once again to the floor.

I landed on my side and lay there. I felt so weak, so frightened. I didn't even try to move.

Panting hard, I waited for the cat to pounce again. Waited to feel its claws wrap around me. Waited to be lifted into the air again.

Waited . . .

When it didn't pounce, I lifted my head. I struggled to focus.

Where was it?

I could hear my brother cheeping in terror somewhere across the floor.

I climbed slowly to my feet. I ruffled my feathers, which were wet and sticky from being inside the cat's mouth.

Where was the cat? Why did it stop torturing me?

The lights flashed on.

"Eeeeep!" I uttered a shrill shriek as a big face lowered itself toward me.

Vanessa!

"Well, well!" her voice boomed in my tiny ears. "What have we here?"

Her hand swooped down and grabbed me off the floor.

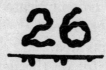

26

She swooped me up, then picked up Cole, too. She perched us in the palm of her hand and held us close to her pale face. A pleased smile spread across her black-lipsticked lips.

"I see you found my spell book, little chickies," she teased. "Let me guess. You must be Crystal and Cole."

Cole and I cheeped loudly and hopped up and down in protest.

Vanessa laughed. "You're both so cute!" she exclaimed. "What a shame I had to teach you a lesson." She tsk-tsked.

"Cheep cheep!" I squeaked.

I wanted to ask why she had done this to Cole and me. I wanted to promise her that no matter what it was we had done — we'd never do it again. I wanted to demand that she change us back — now.

But all I could do was *cheep!*

"What should I do with you two?" Vanessa asked, her dark eyes flashing. "Should I send you back out? It's a long way to your house from here. You'd probably be *eaten* before you got there."

"Cheeeeep!" Cole and I pleaded.

How could we communicate with her? How could we talk to her? How?

I suddenly had an idea.

The old typewriter on the desk. Vanessa was holding Cole and me right above it.

I glanced down. A sheet of white paper lay curled in the typewriter. Yes! I thought. Yes! Our only chance.

I didn't take another second to think about it.

I leaped from Vanessa's palm. And landed with a hard *plop* on the desktop.

"Hey, chickie —!" I heard Vanessa's startled cry. She lowered her hand to pick me up again.

But I jumped onto the typewriter keys. Lowered my head. And began pecking away with my hard little beak.

I pecked a V. Then I hopped up to the left and pecked an A. As Vanessa's hand swooped to grab me, I slid back down to the bottom row and pecked an N.

Vanessa's hand stopped inches above me. Could she see what I was doing? Did she figure out that I was typing her a message?

The E was nearly at the top of the keyboard. I stumbled on the keys and nearly typed the wrong letter. But I hit the E, then backed up a step and pecked two S's.

I glanced up. Yes! She was watching. She had Cole resting in her palm. She leaned over the desk, and her dark eyes stared down at the sheet of paper.

I was gasping for breath by the time I finished. My little heart was pounding. It was such hard work! But I typed the whole message:

VANESSA, WE'RE REALLY SORRY. WE DIDN'T MEAN TO SPILL YOUR GROCERIES. WE CAME TO APOLOGIZE.

I dropped weakly onto the desktop. So exhausted, I could barely move.

I turned and raised my eyes to Vanessa.

Would she help us? Would she accept our apology? Would she change us back to normal?

Vanessa brought her face down close to me. "Your apology is a little too late," she said coldly. "There's nothing I can do."

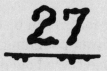

27

Cole uttered a pitiful "Cheep."

I raised myself up with a sigh. Then I stumbled back wearily onto the typewriter keys.

PLEAS, I pecked out.

I was so tired, I didn't have the strength to push down the E at the end.

I gazed up hopefully at Vanessa. She stared down at the word I had typed. She tapped her chin with her black fingernails.

"Well . . ." she said finally. "I like the way you say *'please.'*" She lifted me up gently and set me down in her palm beside Cole.

"Politeness is so important," Vanessa said, holding us up to her face. "Especially for young people. That's what I care about more than anything else in the world. Good manners."

Her dark eyes narrowed at us. "That day in front of the grocery," she scolded, "you didn't apologize for crashing into me. So I had no choice. I had to punish you." She studied us, tsk-tsking.

So *that's* why Anthony wasn't turned into a chicken, too! I realized. Before he ran away, Anthony had called out to Vanessa that he was sorry.

If only Cole and I had apologized then! We wouldn't be peeping little chicks today.

But how were we to know that Vanessa was such a manners freak?

She carried us over to a tall bookshelf and held us close to the books. "Do you see my collection?" she asked. "All etiquette books. Dozens and dozens of manners books. I have dedicated my life to manners."

She gazed at us sternly. "If only kids today weren't so rude. I wish I could help you two. I really do. But your apology came too late. Far too late."

She set us both down on the desk. I guess her hand was getting tired. She rubbed it tenderly with her other hand.

Now what? I wondered.

Was she going to send us home like this? Vanessa was right. Cole and I would never make it. Some dog or cat or raccoon would turn us into dinner before we went a block or two.

I cheeped in panic. My tiny feathers stood straight up. What could we do?

I had one last, desperate idea.

One more time, I climbed onto the typewriter keyboard. And I began to type . . .

THANK YOU FOR EXPLAINING TO US. AND THANK YOU FOR TRYING TO TEACH US TO BE POLITE. YOURS TRULY, COLE AND CRYSTAL

I *said* it was a desperate idea. About as desperate as a chicken can get. But I stared up at Vanessa, watching her read it. Hoping . . . hoping . . .

"I don't *believe* it!" Vanessa exclaimed. She tore the sheet of paper from the typewriter and read it again. "A thank-you note!" she cried. "You wrote me a thank-you note!"

She gazed down at Cole and me with a broad smile. "No kids today *ever* write thank-you notes!" she cried. "This is the politest thing I ever saw!"

She danced around with it. "A thank-you note! An actual thank-you note!"

And then she turned. Pointed a finger at Cole, then at me. Mumbled some words. And pointed again.

"Whooooa!" I cried, feeling my body grow. I felt like a balloon inflating. The little yellow feathers fell away. My hair grew back. My arms . . . my hands!

"YAAAAAY!" I cried. Cole joined my happy cheer.

We were back! Vanessa had changed us back — to *us!*

We pinched each other, just to make sure. Then

we tossed back our heads and laughed. We were so happy!

Vanessa laughed, too. We all laughed gleefully together.

Then Vanessa turned and started toward the kitchen. "Let me get you both a drink," she offered. "I know how thirsty these spells can make a person."

"Thank you!" I cried, remembering how important politeness was to Vanessa.

"Yes — thank you!" Cole added loudly.

We grinned at each other. We pinched each other again. Skin! Real skin — with no feathers!

I moved my lips. I licked them with my tongue. Soft, human lips that didn't click.

Vanessa returned with two glasses of soda. "I know kids like cola," she said. She handed a glass to me and a glass to Cole. "Drink up," she urged. "You've been through a lot."

I *did* feel terribly thirsty. I took a few long sips of the cola. It felt cold and tingly on my tongue. Wonderful! Better than seeds off the carpet.

Wow. I was so happy to be me again.

I raised my eyes and saw Cole tilt his glass to his mouth and drink the soda down. He was really thirsty!

When he finished, he lowered his glass — and let out the loudest burp I ever heard!

Cole burst out laughing.

I couldn't help myself.

It was such a funny burp, I started laughing, too.

I was still laughing when Vanessa stepped in front of me.

What is her problem? I wondered.

Then she pointed her finger, first at Cole, then at me. And whispered, "Pig pig."

About the Author

R.L. Stine is the most popular author in America. He is the creator of the *Goosebumps, Give Yourself Goosebumps, Fear Street*, and *Ghosts of Fear Street* series, among other popular books. He has written more than one hundred scary novels for kids. Bob lives in New York City with his wife, Jane, teenage son, Matt, and dog, Nadine.

Add *more*

to your collection . . .
A chilling preview of
what's next from
R.L. STINE

DON'T GO TO SLEEP!

1

I hate my life.

Pam and Greg use me as their human punching bag. Maybe if Mom were around more, she'd be able to stop them.

But she is hardly ever around. She works two jobs. Her day job is teaching people how to use computers. And her night job is typing at a law firm.

Pam and Greg are supposed to be taking care of me. They take care of me, all right.

They make sure I'm miserable twenty-four hours a day.

"This room stinks," Pam groaned. "Let's get out of here, Greg."

They slammed the door behind them. My model space shuttle fell off the dresser and crashed to the floor.

At least they left me alone. I didn't care what mean things they said, as long as they went away.

I settled on my bed to read *An Attack on*

Pluto. I'd much rather be on the planet Pluto than in my own house—even with giant ants shooting spit rays at me.

My bed felt lumpy. I shoved a bunch of books and clothes to the floor.

I had the smallest bedroom in the house—of course. I always got the worst of everything. Even the guest room was bigger than my room.

I didn't understand it. I needed a big room more than anybody! I had so many books, posters, models, and other junk that there was barely room for me to sleep.

I opened my book and started reading. I came to a really scary part. Justin Case, a human space traveller, was captured by the evil ant emperor. The ant emperor closed in on him, closer, closer. . . .

I shut my eyes for a second—just a second—but I guess I fell asleep. Suddenly I felt the ant emperor's hot, stinking breath on my face!

Ugh! It smelled exactly like dog food.

Then I heard growling.

I opened my eyes.

It was worse than I thought. Worse than an ant emperor.

It was Biggie—ready to spring!

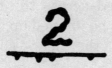

2

"Biggie!" I screamed. "Get off me!"

Snap! He attacked me with his gaping dachshund jaws.

I dodged him—he missed me. I shoved him off the bed.

He snarled at me and tried to jump back up. He was too short. He couldn't reach the bed without taking a running leap.

I stood on the bed. Biggie snapped at my feet. "Help!" I yelled.

That's when I saw Pam and Greg in the doorway, laughing their heads off.

Biggie backed up to take his running jump. "Help me, you guys!" I begged.

"Yeah, right," Pam said. Greg doubled over laughing.

"Come on," I whined. "I can't get down! He'll bite me!"

Greg gasped for breath. "Why do you think we

put him on your bed in the first place? Ha ha ha ha!"

You shouldn't sleep so much, Matt," Greg said. "We thought we had to wake you up."

"Besides, we were bored," Pam added. "We wanted to have some fun."

Biggie galloped across the room and leaped onto the bed. As he jumped up, I jumped down. I scurried across the floor—slipping on comic books as I ran.

Biggie raced after me. I ducked into the hallway and slammed the door just before he got out.

Biggie barked like crazy.

"Let him out, Matt!" Pam scolded me. "How can you be so mean to poor, sweet Biggie?"

"Leave me alone!" I shouted. I ran downstairs to the living room. I plopped myself on the couch and flicked on the TV. I didn't bother to surf—I always watch the same channel. The Sci-Fi channel.

I heard Biggie bounding down the steps. I tensed, waiting for him to attack. But he waddled into the kitchen.

Probably going to eat some disgusting doggie treats, I thought. The fat little monster.

The front door opened. Mom came in, balancing a couple of bags of groceries.

"Hi, Mom!" I cried. I was glad she was home. Pam and Greg cooled it a little when she was around.

"Hi honey." She carried the bags into the kitchen. "There's my little Biggie!" she cooed. "How's my sweet little pup?"

Everybody loves Biggie except for me.

"Greg!" Mom called. "It's your turn to make dinner tonight!"

"I can't!" Greg yelled from upstairs. "Mom—I've got so much homework to do! I can't fix dinner tonight."

Sure. He was so busy doing his homework, he couldn't stop driving me crazy.

"Make Matt do it," Pam shouted. "He's not doing anything. He's just watching TV."

"I have homework too, you know," I protested.

Greg came down the steps. "Right," he said. "Seventh grade homework is *so* tough."

"I'll bet you didn't think it was easy when *you* were in seventh grade."

"Boys, please don't fight," Mom said. "I've only got a couple of hours before I have to go back to work. Matt, start dinner. I'm going to go upstairs and lie down for a few minutes."

I stormed into the kitchen. "Mom! It's not my turn!"

"Greg will cook another night," Mom promised.

"What about Pam?'"

"Matt—that's enough. You're cooking. That's final." She dragged herself upstairs to her bedroom.

"Rats!" I muttered. I opened a cabinet door

and slammed it shut. "I never get my way around here!"

"What are you making for dinner, Matt?" Greg asked. "Geek burgers?"

"Matthew Amsterdam chews with his mouth open." Greg was talking into his stupid tape recorder again. We were all in the kitchen, eating dinner.

"Tonight the Amsterdams have tuna casserole for dinner," he said. "Matt defrosted it. He left it in the oven too long. The noodles on the bottom are burned."

"Shut up," I muttered.

Nobody said anything for a few minutes. The only sounds were forks clicking against plates and Biggie's toenails on the kitchen floor.

"How was school today, kids?" Mom asked.

"Mrs. Amsterdam asks her children about their day," Greg said to the tape recorder.

"Greg, do you have to do that at the dinner table?" Mom sighed.

"Mrs. Amsterdam complains about her son Greg's behavior," Greg murmured.

"Greg!"

"Greg's mother's voice gets louder. Could she be angry?"

"GREG!"

"I have to do it, Mom," Greg insisted in his normal voice. "It's for school!"

"It's getting on my nerves," Mom said.

"Mine, too," I chimed in.

"Who asked you, Matt?" Greg snapped.

"So cut it out until after dinner, okay?" Mom asked.

Greg didnt say anything. But he set the tape recorder on the table and started to eat.

Pam said, "Mom, can I put my winter clothes in the closet in the guest room? My closet is packed."

"I'll think about it," Mom said.

"Hey!" I cried. "She has a huge closet! Her closet is almost as big as my whole room!"

"So?" Pam sneered.

"My room is the smallest one in the house!" I protested. "I can hardly walk through it."

"That's because you're a slob," Pam cracked.

"I'm not a slob! I'm neat! But I need a bigger bedroom. Mom, can I move into the guest room?"

Mom shook her head. "No."

"But why not?"

"I want to keep that room nice for guests," Mom explained.

"What guests?" I cried. "We never have any guests!"

"Your grandparents come every Christmas."

"That's once a year. Grandma and Grandpa won't mind sleeping in my little room once a year. The rest of the time they've got a whole house to themselves!"

"Your room is too small to sleep two people," Mom said. "I'm sorry, Matt. You can't have the guest room."

"Mom!"

"What do you care where you sleep, anyway?" Pam said. "You are the best sleeper in the world. You could sleep through a hurricane!"

Greg picked up the tape recorder. "When Matt isn't propped up in front of the TV, he is usually sleeping. He is asleep more than he's awake."

"Mom, Greg talked into the tape recorder again," I tattled.

"I know," Mom said wearily. "Greg, put it down."

"Mom, please let me switch rooms. I need a bigger room! I don't just sleep in my room—I *live* there! I need a place to get away from Pam and Greg. Mom—you don't know what it's like when you're not here! They're so mean to me!"

"Matt, stop it," Mom replied. "You have a wonderful brother and sister, and they take good care of you. You should appreciate them."

"I hate them!"

"Matt! I've had enough of this! Go to your room!"

"There's no room for me in there!" I cried.

"Now!"

As I ran upstairs to my room, I heard Greg say in his tape recorder voice, "Matt has been punished. His crime? Being a geek."

I slammed the door, stuffed my face in a pillow, and screamed.

I spent the rest of the evening in my room.

"It's not fair!" I muttered to myself. "Pam and Greg get whatever they want—and I get punished!"

Nobody is using the guest room, I thought. I don't care what Mom says. *I'm* sleeping there from now on.

Mom left for her night job. I waited until I heard Pam and Greg turn out the lights and go to their rooms. Then I slipped out of my room and into the guest room.

I was going to sleep in that guest room. And nothing was going to stop me.

I didn't think it was that big a deal. What was the worst thing that could happen? Mom might get mad at me. So what?

I had no idea that when I woke up in the morning, my life would be a complete disaster.

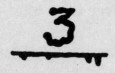

3

My feet were cold. That was the first thing I noticed when I woke up.

They were sticking out from under the covers. I sat up and tossed the blanket down over them.

Then I pulled the blanket back up. Were those my feet?

They were huge. Not monster huge, but huge for me. Way bigger than they'd been the day before.

Man, I thought. I'd heard about growth spurts. I knew kids grew fast at my age. But this was ridiculous!

I crept out of the guest room. I could hear Mom and Pam and Greg downstairs, eating breakfast.

Oh, no, I thought. I slept late. I hope no one noticed that I didn't sleep in my room last night.

I went to the bathroom to brush my teeth. Everything felt a little weird.

When I touched the bathroom doorknob, it seemed to be in the wrong place. As if someone had lowered it during the night. The ceiling felt lower, too.

I turned on the light and glanced in the mirror. Was that me?

I couldn't stop staring at myself. I looked like myself—and I didn't.

My face wasn't so round. I touched my upper lip. It was covered with blond fuzz. And I was about six inches taller than I'd been the day before!

I—I was *older*. I looked about sixteen years old!

No, no, I thought. This can't be right. I've got to be imagining this.

I'll just close my eyes for a minute. When I open them, I'll be twelve again.

I squeezed my eyes shut. I counted to ten.

I opened my eyes.

Nothing had changed.

I was a teenager!

My heart began to pound. I'd read that old story about Rip Van Winkle. He goes to sleep for a hundred years. When he wakes up, everything is different.

Did that happen to me? I wondered. Did I just sleep for four years straight?

You Snooze, You Lose!

Goosebumps®

Cole hates his tiny new bedroom. But when he asks his mom if he can sleep in the guest room she says, "no way." So one night Cole sneaks in. Major mistake! In the morning he wakes up as a teenager. The next day he wakes up as an eighty-year-old man! Now every time he goes to sleep in the guest room, he wakes up in a different body! Will he ever be himself again?

Don't Go to Sleep!

Goosebumps #54

R.L. Stine

Find it at a bookstore near you!

Visit the Web site at http://www.scholastic.com/goosebumps

GBT896

© 1996 Parachute Press, Inc. GOOSEBUMPS is a registered trademark of Parachute Press, Inc. All rights reserved.

CHILLING STORIES BASED ON THE FOX KIDS TV SHOW

R.L. STINE

Goosebumps®

PRESENTS

TV BOOK #11

LET'S GET INVISIBLE!

Max and his friends find an old magic mirror that makes them invisible! But the more they use it, the harder it is to come back.

Then Max realizes that there are people trapped in the mirror! And the only way they can escape is if someone takes their place. Will they take hold of Max? Have they already taken hold of his friends?

With 8 pages of full-color photos from the show!

LOOK FOR IT IN A BOOKSTORE NEAR YOU!

Visit the web site at http://www.scholastic.com/goosebumps

1996 Parachute Press, Inc. GOOSEBUMPS is a registered trademark of Parachute Press, Inc. All rights reserved.   GBTV896

R.L. STINE
GIVE YOURSELF
Goosebumps®

Grandma Goes Galactic!

Your parents are going away and your super-cool grandma is coming to stay with you. But when you go to meet her at the train station you find two grandmas—you see one on the platform—and one inside the train! Which one is the real deal?
If you decide the lady on the platform is Granny, you'll find yourself in the middle of an alien attack!
If you hop on the train, you'll find your real grandma, but she's being watched by aliens!

Pick quick—you've got to rescue Granny and help save the world before your mom and dad get home! Choose from more than 20 eerie endings!

Give Yourself Goosebumps #16
Secret Agent Grandma
by R.L. Stine

Coming to a bookstore near you!

Visit the web site at http://www.scholastic.com/Goosebumps

996 Parachute Press, Inc. GOOSEBUMPS is a registered trademark of Parachute Press, Inc. All rights reserved.   GYGB796

Curly's All-New and Shocking

Only $8.95
Plus $2.00 shipping and handling*

Goosebumps®

Fan Club Pack

Zipper tag

Glow-in-the-Dark Pen

Folder

Game sheets

Wallet

Shipping box

HERE LIES Goosebumps
THE OFFICIAL GOOSEBUMPS FAN CLUB

THE OFFICIAL Goosebumps FAN CLUB
CURLY

Notepad

Curly Bio

From the desk of

CURLY

Unboo-lievable, dudes! It's more exclusive, new Goosebumps stuff to collect! Get the inside scary scoop on the latest books, the TV show, videos, games—and *everything* Goosebumps!

All this plus:
- Game sheets
- Notepad
- Sticker
- A subscription to the official newsletter, *The Scream*

(mailed separately—a few weeks after you receive your pack)

To get your all-new Goosebumps Fan Club Pack (in the U.S. and Canada only), just fill out the coupon below and send it with your check or money order. U.S. residents: $8.95 plus $2.00 shipping and handling to Goosebumps Fan Club, Scholastic Inc., P.O. Box 7500, 2931 East McCarty Street, Jefferson City, MO 65102. Canadian residents: $13.95 plus $2.00 shipping and handling to Goosebumps Fan Club, Scholastic Canada, 123 Newkirk Road, Richmond Hill, Ontario, L4C3G5. Offer expires 9/30/97. Offer good for one year from date of receipt. Please allow 4-6 weeks for your introductory pack to arrive.

*Canadian prices slightly higher. Fan club offer expires 9/30/97. Membership good for one year from date of receipt. Newsletters sent four times during membership.

- -

Hurry! Send me my all-new Goosebumps Fan Club Pack. I am enclosing my check or money order (no cash please) for U.S. residents: $10.95 ($8.95 plus $2.00) and for Canadian residents: $15.95 ($13.95 plus $2.00).

Name_____Birthdate _____

Address_____

City_____State_____Zip_____

Telephone (   )_____Boy_____Girl_____

Where did you buy this book? ☐ Bookstore ☐ Book Fair ☐ Book Club ☐ Other

1996 Parachute Press, Inc. GOOSEBUMPS is a registered trademark of Parachute Press, Inc. All Rights Reserved.

GB53397

GOT Goosebumps® YET?

by R.L. Stine

——— GOOSEBUMPS ———

☐ BAB45365-3	#1	Welcome to Dead House	$3.99
☐ BAB45366-1	#2	Stay Out of the Basement	$3.99
☐ BAB45367-X	#3	Monster Blood	$3.99
☐ BAB45368-8	#4	Say Cheese and Die!	$3.99
☐ BAB45369-6	#5	The Curse of the Mummy's Tomb	$3.99
☐ BAB49445-7	#10	The Ghost Next Door	$3.99
☐ BAB49450-3	#15	You Can't Scare Me!	$3.99
☐ BAB47742-0	#20	The Scarecrow Walks at Midnight	$3.99
☐ BAB48355-2	#25	Attack of the Mutant	$3.99
☐ BAB48348-X	#30	It Came from Beneath the Sink	$3.99
☐ BAB48349-8	#31	The Night of the Living Dummy II	$3.99
☐ BAB48344-7	#32	The Barking Ghost	$3.99
☐ BAB48345-5	#33	The Horror at Camp Jellyjam	$3.99
☐ BAB48346-3	#34	Revenge of the Lawn Gnomes	$3.99
☐ BAB48340-4	#35	A Shocker on Shock Street	$3.99
☐ BAB56873-6	#36	The Haunted Mask II	$3.99
☐ BAB56874-4	#37	The Headless Ghost	$3.99
☐ BAB56875-2	#38	The Abominable Snowman of Pasadena	$3.99
☐ BAB56876-0	#39	How I Got My Shrunken Head	$3.99
☐ BAB56877-9	#40	Night of the Living Dummy III	$3.99
☐ BAB56878-7	#41	Bad Hare Day	$3.99
☐ BAB56879-5	#42	Egg Monsters from Mars	$3.99
☐ BAB56880-9	#43	The Beast from the East	$3.99
☐ BAB56881-7	#44	Say Cheese and Die–Again!	$3.99
☐ BAB56882-5	#45	Ghost Camp	$3.99
☐ BAB56883-3	#46	How to Kill a Monster	$3.99
☐ BAB56884-1	#47	Legend of the Lost Legend	$3.99
☐ BAB56885-X	#48	Attack of the Jack-O'-Lanterns	$3.99
☐ BAB56886-8	#49	Vampire Breath	$3.99
☐ BAB56887-6	#50	Calling All Creeps	$3.99
☐ BAB56888-4	#51	Beware, the Snowman	$3.99
☐ BAB56889-2	#52	How I Learned to Fly	$3.99

——— GOOSEBUMPS PRESENTS ———

☐ BAB74586-7	TV Episode #1: The Girl Who Cried Monster	$3.99
☐ BAB74587-5	TV Episode #2: The Cuckoo Clock of Doom	$3.99
☐ BAB74588-3	TV Episode #3: Welcome to Camp Nightmare	$3.99
☐ BAB74589-1	TV Episode #4: Return of the Mummy	$3.99
☐ BAB74590-5	TV Episode #5: Night of the Living Dummy II	$3.99
☐ BAB82519-4	TV Episode #6: My Hairiest Adventure	$3.99

© 1996 Parachute Press, Inc. GOOSEBUMPS is a registered trademark of Parachute Press, Inc. All rights reserved.

❏ BAB93954-8	TV Episode #7: My Hairiest Adventure	$3.99
❏ BAB93955-6	TV Episode #8: Be Careful What You Wish For	$3.99
❏ BAB93959-9	TV Episode #9: Go Eat Worms!	$3.99
❏ BAB62836-4	Tales to Give You Goosebumps Book & Light Set Special Edition #1	$11.95
❏ BAB26603-9	More Tales to Give You Goosebumps Book & Light Set Special Edition #2	$11.95
❏ BAB74150-4	Even More Tales to Give You Goosebumps Book and Boxer Shorts Pack Special Edition #3	$14.99

—————————— GIVE YOURSELF GOOSEBUMPS ——————————

❏ BAB55323-2	#1: Escape from the Carnival of Horrors	$3.99
❏ BAB56645-8	#2: Tick Tock, You're Dead	$3.99
❏ BAB56646-6	#3: Trapped in Bat Wing Hall	$3.99
❏ BAB67318-1	#4: The Deadly Experiments of Dr. Eeek	$3.99
❏ BAB67319-X	#5: Night in Werewolf Woods	$3.99
❏ BAB67320-3	#6: Beware of the Purple Peanut Butter	$3.99
❏ BAB67321-1	#7: Under the Magician's Spell	$3.99
❏ BAB84765-1	#8: The Curse of the Creeping Coffin	$3.99
❏ BAB84766-X	#9: The Knight in Screaming Armor	$3.99
❏ BAB84767-8	#10: Diary of a Mad Mummy	$3.99
❏ BAB84768-6	#11: Deep in the Jungle of Doom	$3.99
❏ BAB84772-4	#12: Welcome to the Wicked Wax Museum	$3.99
❏ BAB84773-2	#13: Scream of the Evil Genie	$3.99
❏ BAB84774-0	#14: The Creepy Creations of Professor Shock	$3.99

❏ BAB53770-9	The Goosebumps Monster Blood Pack	$11.95
❏ BAB50995-0	The Goosebumps Monster Edition #1	$12.95
❏ BAB93371-X	The Goosebumps Monster Edition #2	$12.95
❏ BAB60265-9	Goosebumps Official Collector's Caps Collecting Kit	$5.99
❏ BAB73906-9	Goosebumps Postcard Book	$7.95
❏ BAB73902-6	The 1997 Goosebumps 365 Scare-a-Day Calendar	$8.95
❏ BAB73907-7	The Goosebumps 1997 Wall Calendar	$10.99

Scare me, thrill me, mail me GOOSEBUMPS now!

Available wherever you buy books, or use this order form. Scholastic Inc., P.O. Box 7502,
2931 East McCarty Street, Jefferson City, MO 65102

Please send me the books I have checked above. I am enclosing $_____ (please add $2.00 to cover shipping and handling). Send check or money order — no cash or C.O.D.s please.

Name _____ Age _____

Address _____

City _____ State/Zip_____

Please allow four to six weeks for delivery. Offer good in the U.S. only. Sorry, mail orders are not available to residents of Canada. Prices subject to change.